MONDAY'S MURDERER

MADIGAN AMOS ZOO MYSTERIES

RUBY LOREN

BRITISH AUTHOR

Please note, this book is written in British English and contains British spellings.

BOOKS IN THE SERIES

T he dead man didn't have a name.

He'd had one once, like everyone else, but a lot of things had come to pass since he'd been born, thirty two years previously. He'd dabbled in many different businesses during his time, and it was surely one of these 'businesses' which had come back around to bite him.

He lay on his back with a pool of red spreading out from beneath him, courtesy of the dagger that had been thrust into his back. His eyes stared sightlessly up at the stars, oblivious to the happy day of celebrations that was still ongoing just a few miles down the road from his final resting place. Dead men have no need for weddings.

After he'd lain there unmoving for a while and the sound of his killer's footsteps had finally faded into nothing, his new neighbour made her tentative approach. The smell of blood and fresh meat made her nostrils flare a little. She crept forwards, acknowledging the scent of death and concluding that this was surely just another meal. Someone else had already been at work on the man's face, but she didn't care. She missed the taste of fresh meat and, although she hadn't been the one to kill this new prey, the still-warm corpse appealed to her more than any of the party tricks that had been set up in her enclosure to encourage her to work for her food. They were always things long dead. They were food. This was different. This was life.

She crunched down on an arm, feeling her teeth slide through flesh and into bone. Her yellow eyes remained fixed on what was left of the man's face, but he made no move. Satisfied once and for all that her prey really was dead, the lynx got to work.

MARRIAGE AND MURDER

E veryone claims that their wedding day is the happiest day of their life. For me, it was definitely one of the best, but I'd been blessed with so many happy experiences that I couldn't pin it all on one day. It was, however, a day that made me remember all of those other days, and the happiness they'd brought. The people who had given me such wonderful memories and happy times were all present to celebrate my joining with Auryn.

The zoo restaurant, now renamed The Wild Spot and operating as a separate entity from Avery Zoo, had always been renovated with my wedding to Auryn in mind. Astonishingly, our marriage wasn't even the first wedding to take place at my new restaurant. Two couples had managed to squeeze in last minute arrangements before our mid-October nuptials.

I might be biased, but I thought that our wedding was by far the most magical. My best friend Tiff and all of her shop employees had been out in force, tying up decorations and arranging autumnal wreaths. Both Auryn and I had been relegated to working at The Lucky Zoo for the day before our marriage, so we couldn't see what was being done as the staff had announced that all of this setting up would be their present to us.

Auryn and I hadn't expected a huge fuss to be made, and therefore hadn't arranged for anything like flowers, but after Tiff had failed to cajole me into doing some decent planning, she'd finally come up with this new solution. When we'd arrived at The Wild Spot to find it covered with autumnal wreaths and garlands and with the smell of cinnamon and roasting chestnuts in the air, I was gladder than ever to have such wonderful friends.

The wedding itself had gone off without too many hitches. Rameses and Lucky (our pet dog and pet cat) were the ring bearers. Rameses had come straight to me when Auryn had called him (he was particularly attached to me for some reason) but that was better than Lucky had managed. For a cat, Lucky was supposed to be well-trained, but he was still very prone to, well - 'cattiness'. When I'd called him to bring Auryn's ring forwards I'd had to delve into my bouquet and pull out the pack of treats I'd concealed there, knowing that Lucky managed to be particularly hard of hearing when he wanted to be. One crinkle of the plastic was enough to get him running towards us, and at least it had caused plenty of amusement amongst our guests.

Beyond that, things had been perfect. No one had fallen over, no one had spoken up with a shock reason against our being married, and even my elusive parents had made the trip over for the special day. As time wore on into the evening and we launched into the zoo-themed games - both of our zoos' staff had come up with them when Tiff had asked what they thought made a good wedding, I couldn't have been happier.

After a particularly energetic scavenger hunt, which had made me glad I'd chosen a short dress (I was so small, the long ones I'd tried had made me look like a tiny meringue) I settled down with my signature 'hippos in mud' hot chocolate from the restaurant's menu and breathed in the smell of woodsmoke in the autumn air. It had been a bright sunny day.

It had been a perfect day.

"We're married. I can't believe it," Auryn said, voicing my own thoughts aloud.

"Any regrets?" I asked him with a sideways smile.

"None," he told me.

I leant over and kissed my husband.

"There's only one thing I'm sorry about," he said when we broke apart. I raised my eyebrows at him. "The way I see it, your generous gesture of having an 'open restaurant' means that your profits will have taken a hit. You're going to fall behind on our little bet. It's such a shame." He tried to look sorry and failed.

"Don't worry about it. The owner gave me a good rate, but I think it's fair for all involved. My parents practically forced me to let them pay," I replied with my own sideways smile.

"You're billing them for the restaurant you own? That's shameless!"

"Of course I'm not! I told them that their paying for the air fare over was more than enough of a present. It's just good to see them again. We argued, and they finally agreed that you and I will pay the bill. So that's settled!"

Auryn took a moment to process it. "You're serious, aren't you?"

I grinned. "Just because one of us owns the business doesn't mean we get freebies."

"Well in that case… I want a fee for closing Avery Zoo all day. I deserve compensation!"

I couldn't keep the act up any longer. "Now who's taking our bet too seriously?"

He looked at me and finally realised I'd been pulling his leg all along. "I'm still going to win," he informed me. "Halloween is just around the corner and the horror zoo events are already bringing in the crowds."

"The Halloween menu has been a hit, too. You won't believe how popular autumnal weddings are either. People will pay through the roof..." I replied, hinting that I was doing just as well.

I'd finally relented and shown Auryn the zoo's and restaurant's financials, when he'd complained that it wasn't fair that I had access to both. After some reflection, and a look at the forecasts, we'd both concluded that it was going to be a close-fought thing. There was no way of knowing who would be the first across the line. The Lucky Zoo had more money to pay off, but it had more cash coming in every day. By comparison, the restaurant needed less money, but it was limited by its size. I had no idea who was going to win.

Auryn had accused me of actually paying for the food and drink I habitually took from the restaurant (and therefore singlehandedly pushing the restaurant into profit) but I'd vehemently denied those charges. Half of the point of having your own restaurant was the free food, and my chef, Connie, spoiled me.

"We never actually discussed the consequences for the loser of this bet," I mused.

"I assumed it was gloating rights for the winner." Auryn gave me that same smile that had the effect of making me fall in love with him all over again every time he used it.

"Of course, but maybe we should think of something else." I waggled my eyebrows at him.

"How dare you! I'm a married man you know." An evil

grin suddenly lit up Auryn's face. "What about the loser gets the peacocks and Bernard the turkey?"

I shot him a glare. "Don't you try and palm them off on me again. They were your mistake!"

"Aren't you confident that you can win? If you were confident, you wouldn't mind raising the stakes…"

I shook my head at him. The peacocks and Bernard had haunted my zoo for longer than I'd wanted, when a lynx had been stalking Avery Zoo's fowl collection. Auryn had done everything he could to avoid taking them back, but after one stressful chase around the elephant enclosure with the pack of peacocks hot on my heels, I'd finally snapped. After clothing ourselves in as near to bullet-proof gear as we could find, I and a team of less than willing zookeepers had bundled the peacocks and Bernard into a crate which had then been delivered to Avery Zoo at the dead of night.

Auryn had not been best pleased to discover the peacocks had made their return, but he could hardly argue now that they were back home. He was the one who'd taken them on in the first place, against my better judgement.

"So, it's a deal then?" Auryn wheedled.

I shook my head very seriously at him before waving at my parents, who were in the middle of chatting to Tiff. I spared a thought to wonder what they were discussing, but the amused looks they were shooting in my direction let me know that Tiff was filling them in on the truth about their famous daughter. I suspected it wasn't all favourable either.

Normally, I'd have jokingly told her off for it at a later date, but I didn't know how to treat Tiff at the moment. On the day of her own wedding, only a month previously, I'd discovered that her new husband was not the man she thought him to be. A good friend would have told Tiff the truth, but I hadn't been able to do it. I hadn't wanted to ruin her day, or her life. And anyway… what did I really know for sure? I'd told myself I needed some more time to get to the bottom of who, exactly, Alex Gregory was, but as yet, I hadn't made any progress. I knew that it didn't justify not telling Tiff, and that there would certainly be consequences, but I still couldn't bring myself to do it.

Feeling terrible, I'd confided in Auryn, as he usually sensed the right thing to do when it came to people, but my usually sensitive partner had clammed up just the way I had. Sharing the burden of guilt made me feel a little less bad, but it was still guilt - no matter how thinly you tried to spread it.

I shook my head free of the negative thoughts. Detective Gregory wasn't here today, and I was glad of it. He'd been invited, but some essential police training course had come up. Privately, I assumed he wanted to avoid my wedding, and probably wished I'd done the same for him. Ever since I'd witnessed him pulling a gun on a home invader, he'd behaved differently around me. There was something unspoken between us. I thought he believed I'd guessed the truth about him… whatever it may actually be.

"I forgot to mention… Tiff told me that the crazy guy who broke into her house has been stripped of whatever rank he had in the police force. I think he was a detective in Brighton - where Alex worked," Auryn said, somehow managing to follow my thoughts exactly.

"No jail time?"

Auryn shook his head. "Tiff said they're treating it like some kind of mental breakdown. I suppose no harm was actually done…"

I frowned. Auryn hadn't been there that night. Jim Smith had wanted to do a great deal of harm to my best friend and to anyone who'd got in his way. I may not know everything about Alex Gregory's history, but I was still grateful that he'd been in the house.

One person I was sorry was missing the event was my

friend, Katya. Katya worked for MI5, but in spite of all that, we'd developed a friendship, and I found I'd come to rely on her both for her expert advice and her companionship. I thought she felt the same way about me, but as so often happened, her work made it so she wasn't able to be here today. Upon reflection, it would hardly have been prudent either. Katya and I were not supposed to be friends as far as the powers-that-be were concerned.

"Are we still on for our post-wedding ride tomorrow?" Auryn asked, shooting me a hopeful look.

I watched the flames dance for a moment before I summoned up what I hoped was a convincing smile. "Nothing would make me happier!"

"You need to work on that," he said, nudging me lightly in the ribs.

After a local estate agent had been arrested for double murder, Auryn had agreed to take on the care of the killer's horse and the horse of one of the victims. Harry Farley's last will and testament had decreed that all of this family money went to a charity dedicated to preserving wildlife. Although his wife was still arguing the toss, it looked to be legally binding. Poor Felicity Farley was the butt of a joke played on Harry by his ex-wife, Georgina Farley. I privately thought that it served Harry right for messing with a lawyer, but I was sure that neither side had been guiltless. I wanted to feel sorry for Felicity, but her character made that very hard to do.

The result of it was that we'd ended up with a pair of horses, who were apparently itching to tear about the coun-tryside over hedges and across fields... and that meant we had to ride them. To say I was not a natural horsewoman was an understatement. The dappled grey gelding I'd been saddled with was a handful and a half, but while Auryn's horse, Columbia, was quieter, he was much too large for someone of my size to ride. To be honest, I thought that Smoke-in-the-Woods (Smokey, to us common folk) was too big for me, too, but Auryn assured me that my personality more than made up for it. I wasn't convinced.

"Are you sure you married the right woman?" I muttered.

"No use trying to wriggle out of it now. You said 'I do'," he reminded me. "I'm pretty sure there was something in those wedding vows that means you can't say no to going riding with me, as well."

"We must be remembering them differently," I sniped back.

"You'll enjoy it one day… just wait and see."

I sighed, privately wondering how many falls it would take before I started to 'enjoy' it. I'd suggested swapping Smokey with Merrylegs - one of Avery Zoo's Shetland ponies - but apparently people would have noticed, and giant hunters didn't have the same cute appeal that small furry ponies did.

"If I break my neck and can't do this next consulting job, I will kill you," I told him, half serious.

Auryn rolled his eyes. "Don't be a drama queen. You know, that's why I think you and Smokey get on so well… you're both flouncy."

"I am not flouncy!" I spluttered, outraged by that description.

Auryn just smiled in an infuriating manner that meant I was proving him right, even as I protested. "One little ride and then we'll be working our first official consulting job together."

I smiled a little at that thought. Auryn and I had worked at a zoo together before, but this was the first time it had been planned and arranged in advance. It was also the first time that I'd reached out to a zoo, rather than the other way around, but there was an excellent reason for it.

With the help of my ex-literary agent (now going by the name of Joe Harvey) I'd discovered that there was a huge animal smuggling operation taking place in Great Britain, and it had been happening under my very nose. Auryn's father had been caught selling zoo animals on the black market to private collectors, but I'd never dreamed that there were other zoos doing the same... and worse.

According to Joe, who was well-versed in these things having a background as a member of an international money-laundering operation, there were a lot of zoos involved in shipping animals out of the country. Theoretically, the same smugglers shipped animals into Britain, too, but it was the zoos and their illegal trade that really horrified me. I had firsthand experience of how they could cook the books. Animals could be listed as deceased due to sudden illness, offspring could be incorrectly added up... the list of dirty tactics went on. It all amounted to animals disappearing without anyone batting an eyelid.

But I was determined to put a stop to it.

Joe had given me a tip off about a large zoo that was allegedly profiting from this illegal trade. Auryn and I had hatched a plan. We'd pitched our services to the zoo... and they'd accepted. I'd wanted to waste no time in putting an end to the terrible trade, which was why we started work there in a day's time.

Auryn and I had already agreed that a honeymoon was unnecessary. Our last holiday had been anything but quiet, and who needed a holiday from our job, anyway? We were both happiest when we were at work, doing what we loved.

"Here's to the end of animal smugglers and corrupt zoos," Auryn said, solemnly passing me a marshmallow on a stick, taken from the big pile that had been left at the centre of the picnic bench.

"Cheers," I said, echoing the toast, before the joy of the

day returned and we fought over space in the flames. Auryn's first marshmallow was incinerated. After much giggling, and the further loss of some marshmallows, we toasted our treats in a fuzzy and content sort of silence, thinking only of our own happiness.

We were blissfully clueless that just a few miles away at The Lucky Zoo, a man lay dead in the lynx enclosure.

When the last few guests were leaving the zoo that night, Auryn and I thanked Tiff for her hard work. She told us not to mention it, before leading us to her car, which was all done up with ribbons. As well as organising most of the event after I'd catastrophically failed to get into 'the wedding mood' she'd offered to be our taxi home, too. It was only when we were driving away that I remembered I'd forgotten something important.

"Tiff… can we swing by The Lucky Zoo?" I casually asked as we drove along the country lanes.

She made eye contact with me in the rearview mirror and I pulled a guilty face. She would immediately guess that I'd forgotten my wedding present to Auryn - the one we'd spent so much time working on together. It was something I tended to think of as sweet sentimental rubbish, and I'd said as much when Tiff had suggested the idea, but once I'd got into it, I'd changed my mind.

With Tiff's help, we'd compiled a book for Auryn that was the 'adventure map' of our relationship. I'd drawn the comic sketches of some of my favourite funny zoo anecdotes, some of which I'd already used in my comic, *Monday's Menagerie*. I'd redrawn them truthfully this time - including Auryn and me as the characters.

Tiff had drawn maps of both of our zoos and included

quirky comments on events that had taken place and things that lurked… like the peacocks. I'd been thrilled when the final version had been delivered, and although we'd agreed no presents, I'd always intended to give Auryn my gift to him after the wedding. Except that I'd forgotten it. In my mind, I could see it still sitting on the desk in my office at The Lucky Zoo, right where I'd left it the previous evening.

"Is anything wrong?" Auryn asked, looking concerned that there might be an animal emergency.

I shot a 'help me' look at Tiff.

"Nothing's wrong. Earlier in the evening, a keeper who was doing the nightly round noticed that she didn't count all of the raccoons in the enclosure. There's a chance that Billy's escaped, but she couldn't be sure…" she said.

"Typical! He always picks his moment," Auryn complained, shaking his head at the mention of the wayward raccoon.

I threw a grateful look in Tiff's direction. She'd managed to come up with something entirely too plausible. Billy was another nightmare that Auryn had tried to farm off on someone else. Unfortunately, by a twist of fate, that someone had ended up being me.

"I won't be a minute. I'm sure that she just didn't count up right," I said, slipping out of the car as soon as we arrived in the car park outside of my zoo.

Billy had actually remained in captivity for a startling amount of time. I almost felt bad about removing his tools for constructing ways to escape, but I wasn't about to forget the trouble he liked to get into when he did manage to get out. None of the other raccoons felt the need to escape from their lovely, large enclosure, but Billy had always been a little bit different. I thought that this time I might have finally flummoxed him.

It only took me a couple of minutes to go up to my office

and collect the forgotten book. Then, because I'd managed to psych myself out with all of this talk of Billy, I took a circuitous route back to the car, just to make sure that he really was still inside his enclosure.

It was the crunching sounds that first drew my attention to the lynx enclosure. Liberty (named after her brief spell of freedom) was the zoo's newest resident. She'd settled in nicely and I'd been looking into finding her a mate, or at least a friend, to share her enclosure with, but for now, she lived alone. I knew that she'd been fed earlier in the evening. I assumed she must be gnawing on a bone, left over from a previous meal.

I walked over, still dressed in my wedding dress and with a silly carefree smile on my face. The stars were bright tonight, and I found that I was afforded an excellent view of Liberty… and what she was chewing on.

"Oh no," I said aloud, realising that there was a body in the lynx enclosure. My mind ran a thousand possibilities as I stared in horror at the surprise snack that had fallen into the lynx's clutches. Had someone broken into the zoo, fallen in, and then been attacked by the lynx? The poor man's face looked like it had been mauled but… I frowned, recognising the shirt that the victim wore. It was made by a small designer that the man in the lynx enclosure had once worked with, in his past life, as another creative cover for his money laundering operation.

Someone had finally caught up with Joe Harvey.

PRIOR KNOWLEDGE

Detective Gregory was first on the scene with the usual gaggle of forensics and other police officers. I'd called the police as soon as I'd returned to the car and explained to Tiff and Auryn what I'd discovered. My lovely wedding present to Auryn had been placed in the backseat, forgotten, and we'd all steeled ourselves. All three of us knew the truth of Joe Harvey's identity. That meant that all three of us knew how much trouble we were in. If they found out who he really was, this case wasn't going to be a local police matter. It was going to involve British Intelligence. And they would be furious when they found out the truth.

"You believe you know the identity of the victim?" Detective Gregory was saying.

I blinked a little and adjusted my glasses (gold-rimmed for the special occasion). "Yes, I believe it's Joe Harvey. He worked for the zoo as a marketing and PR expert." *Darn good he'd been at it, too!* I thought, ruefully. I may have always doubted his true motives for wanting a 'proper' job, but I couldn't deny that he'd been terribly successful getting both the restaurant and the zoo a lot of business. He would be much missed.

"What makes you think it's him?" the detective pressed, shooting a skeptical look over at the body when he said it.

I didn't bother looking again. I'd already seen more than enough of what had been done to Joe. When the police had arrived, the first thing I'd had to do was get the lynx into her sleeping quarters and away from the body, so that forensics and the police could safely enter the enclosure. It had taken a lot of bribery and some skilful cat-enticing movements to convince her to come. I'd been reminded that this lynx had been a master of evading capture. As sickening as it was, it was clear that she hadn't forgotten the taste of fresh meat.

"I recognised his shirt," I said, simply.

The detective didn't look convinced, but he nodded anyway.

I was too tired to explain further. This day had been so perfect, and I couldn't help but feel a bit resentful that it had been messed up by a murder.

I must have accidentally muttered something along those lines because the detective shot me a cold look. "What makes you think that it's murder?"

"What makes you think that it's not? Joe wasn't an idiot. He would never have gone into the lynx enclosure. He doesn't even have anything to do with the animals. Also, his face…" I frowned and was then able to catch up with where my thoughts were taking me. "Those marks were supposed to look like claw marks, but they were done by someone who doesn't know anything about big cats. Their claws tear - they don't cut. Whatever was done to his face was done with something sharp, like a knife."

The detective looked interested now. Too interested. I'd clearly said something suspicious.

"Was there a knife involved?" I asked, not wanting to play guessing games.

"This man was stabbed in the back," the detective confirmed.

"Someone probably wanted to send a message," I said, before I remembered who I was talking to.

The detective's eyebrows shot up in surprise. I couldn't help but wonder if he was acting. "Did this man have many enemies?"

"Oh, he upset a lot of other PR companies and web gurus," I said, taking a leaf from Joe's own book by telling some of the truth, but not all of it.

"I'll have someone investigate that," the detective assured me, before looking uncomfortable.

I found I was able to read his mind. "Did your course finish early?"

"It, uh… was cancelled, actually. I didn't want to ruin your guest numbers, so I decided not to come. I hope that was okay?" He looked genuinely conflicted.

"I understand. That was thoughtful of you, but it would have been no trouble," I assured him, keeping a pleasant smile on my face. Inside, I felt like a pit had opened up, ready to swallow me whole.

Detective Alex Gregory hadn't been on a course when he'd been called to the crime scene.

He hadn't been at my wedding.

He didn't have an alibi.

"Why do you think someone picked the lynx enclosure to put him in? I see the 'how' is quite obvious…" The detective nodded his head in the direction of the ladder that had been propped up against the living wall of the enclosure. I recognised it as being one that lived in the old garages the Abraham family had built behind their barn conversion. It wasn't the kind of thing that a newcomer to the zoo would idly pick up and use, but I was already convinced that whoever had done this knew The Lucky Zoo quite well.

They'd chosen the lynx enclosure for a reason. They wanted to send a message. Those in the know would understand that Joe had stuck his nose into the wrong person's business, and it had cost him his life. We were supposed to believe that the person in question was something to do with the animal smuggling gang we were investigating, but I wasn't convinced. The smugglers would have known about the lynx, but not the ladder. It still didn't narrow my options down too greatly, as both Detective Gregory, the entire zoo staff, and a great number of British Intelligence agents had all spent time at the zoo. Any one of them would have known where the ladders were kept.

I bit my tongue, wondering how to proceed. I didn't trust Detective Gregory, not by a long shot, but I also didn't want to lie to him - especially when it could help solve Joe's murder.

I made a decision, hoping I could tell some, but not all. "That lynx probably originated from a zoo up in Scotland."

The detective nodded. He must have heard that much when the case was being investigated.

"Joe believed there might be something fishy going on at the zoo. We were looking into the lynx case together. However, as far as I know, there's no actual proof anything untoward was going on," I said with a little shrug. That was the truth. Joe had never offered me any proof, but I'd believed him completely. Crazy though it might sound, I'd ended up trusting the man. "But please, if you can… keep that information to yourself? I don't think it's actually relevant to the case. It's just what you're supposed to think."

The detective was looking more confused by the second. "What I'm supposed to think?"

"Yes… I believe the killer knows this zoo," I told him and quickly explained about the ladder.

"That may be a logical explanation," he acknowledged. "But that doesn't rule out this supposed animal-related foul play. Surely the lynx enclosure is evidence enough of that? Do you know what he was doing to try to uncover the truth?"

I shook my head. "I just don't think it's to do with the suspicious zoo…" *But it is to do with someone who knows about it,* I silently added to myself. "I'm actually about to start work trying to look into the claims Joe made. I would be so grateful if you were able to keep all of this under your hat. I understand that it's a murder investigation, but just… could you keep it between people you trust?" I hated having to put my faith in a man whom I didn't trust myself, but what choice did I have? Even though I wasn't confiding the entire truth to the detective, it would still be enough to spark suspicions if the press got hold of it.

The detective sighed and looked ten years older for a moment. "We'll have to look into every possibility," he said. "First things first, we'll have to identify him. I know you said you recognised the shirt he's wearing, but we're going to need more confirmation than that."

I nodded, not thinking properly about what he'd just said. One of the forensics team was waving frantically. If I hadn't been so distracted I'd have realised what he meant… and how much trouble that put me in.

"What is it?" Alex asked, striding over.

I trotted along behind him, equally curious.

Tiff and Auryn rejoined me on the walk, having spoken to other officers about how we'd all come to be at the zoo at this late hour… and dressed for a wedding.

"It's a legal document that refers to a publishing contract. I don't know why he would have been carrying it around," the female forensic investigator was saying when I caught up with the detective. She stopped talking and stared at me. Then she clammed up.

"It's something to do with me, isn't it?" I said, having the benefit of the knowledge that the dead man had once been my literary agent.

The forensic investigator exchanged a significant look with Detective Gregory who turned to me. "I think we should discuss it down at the station."

"Oh, must we do it now?" Tiff protested. "It's their wedding night!"

The detective looked mollified, but explained to his new wife that it was a murder investigation, and therefore it did have to be right now.

It was all I could do to not sigh and roll my eyes. If they knew everything I did, they'd realise that this whole set-up was a farce. Someone was playing with them. Unfortunately, the killer was probably just as aware as I was that I could hardly tell them the truth. Everything was going just the way Joe's killer had planned, and I would have to buckle down for a bumpy ride.

"Are you going to tell me more about the document in Joe Harvey's pocket?" I asked when we were finally sitting in an interrogation room at the police station. I'd seen the inside of it enough times that I thought I probably knew my way around as well as any member of staff.

Detective Gregory studied me for a moment before he spoke. "To my untrained eye, it appears to be a document from Rock and Roll Publishing stating that your contract with them is not to be dissolved. It's dated earlier this year. If memory serves, it's from around the time you found a new publisher." He cleared his throat, clearly embarrassed to be party to that information. I hoped that Tiff was the one who'd told him. Otherwise, I wasn't sure I wanted to find out why he knew so much about my comic book career.

"I can assure you that my contract with Rock and Roll Publishing was dissolved legally. To tell the truth, I'm not sure what happened to the company. They seemed to vanish off the face of the map." I kept a straight face, knowing that I could be in conversation with a man who knew a lot more about the truth than he was letting on.

"Do you have any idea why your..." he consulted his notes "...zoo PR and marketing guru might have been carrying a legal document relating to your old publishers?"

"That's a question I'd like to know the answer to, too," I diplomatically replied. "I don't know why he would have had it," I added, knowing that the detective would want something more definite. It was the truth. I'd had no idea that such a document had existed, and I had even less of a clue as to why it had been on Joe's person when he'd met his nasty end.

Other than the obvious - that his killer had wanted it to be found.

"Had anyone signed the document?" I asked, trying to sound offhand about it. If Joe's other name - the one I'd known him by first - was written on it, that could definitely complicate matters.

"It was signed by a Leona Dresden. Do you know her?"

"I met her once. She was in charge of the whole company, so that does make sense." I frowned. "I still don't know why she'd have signed something like that. My contract was dissolved." Of that much I was certain. All of the legal documentation had been sent to me via courier on the same day that MI5 had made their move on the fake publishing company - only to find they'd slipped through their fingers.

"No contact details I suppose?" Detective Gregory

sounded even more tired than the late hour warranted. I was feeling rather tired myself and none too sober either. It was my wedding day and I'd had a fabulous time, oblivious that the night would end this way.

"Nope. I don't think there's anything more I can say. I'll be happy to come back when you've investigated further," I said, with a pointed look down at my wedding dress.

The detective had the good grace to look guilty. "Yes, of course. Someone will give you a call." There was an expression on his face that made me realise there was something on the tip of his tongue. "I'm sorry I didn't come to your wedding. I just thought... Tiff's your best friend. You wouldn't want me there when we don't exactly have the best history." He cleared his throat, aware that he was digging himself deeper into the hole rather than out of it.

"You would have been welcome," I replied, hoping that it was a soft reprimand that would make an end to things.

"I guess I also figured that, if I stayed away, maybe no bodies would turn up..." he muttered under his breath - but loudly enough that I could hear it - as we walked out of the interrogation room. I decided to forget it. Now wasn't the time to pick a fight with Detective Gregory. I had my doubts about him, and I was sure as heck going to be satisfying my curiosity, but a murder had taken place... and it was my wedding day! Seeing as I was definitely not the one responsible for putting that knife in Joe's back, I saw no reason why this all couldn't be put on hold until tomorrow.

I walked back through the police station hoping I'd done enough to cover up the truth, whilst staying honest where I could. I was walking a fine line, and I knew what would happen if the truth got out. I'd already decided that the best thing that could happen would be for Joe's murder to go unsolved and for the whole thing to blow over. There was no need to get *them* involved. With a bit of luck, they'd never find out about the murder.

Auryn was waiting in the reception area with Tiff when I came out. Their own questioning had apparently been briefer than mine, which wasn't surprising. They weren't on the list of suspected murderers due to a very incriminating piece of evidence.

"Are you okay?" Tiff asked, anguish written across her face.

I found I felt sorrier for her than I did for myself. She and her team of workers had put so much time and effort into making today perfect, and then I'd carelessly stumbled across a corpse. "I'm fine. Definitely time for bed," I told her with the best smile I could manage.

"I'm sorry about Joe," she said as we exited the station. Her eyes slid across to mine, curiously, and I knew she was silently asking if I knew anything more about his death than I'd revealed to the authorities. Tiff may be married to a detective, but when Auryn and I had told her about Joe's true identity, she'd agreed that it was safer for everyone if we kept that information to ourselves.

At least - it had seemed safer up until now.

We were silent until safely back on the road and driving for home.

"What's the game plan?" Auryn asked in morose tones once we were clear of the police station.

"I think it will be safest to pretend that Joe pulled the wool over our eyes. After all, if he hadn't all but told me who he really was, I might never have figured it out myself." I didn't actually believe that was true. Once I'd employed him for a while, I was certain I'd have recognised his mannerisms and trademark dark sense of humour. You could change everything about your appearance, but it was a lot harder to change the person inside. And unless I was much mistaken, Joe's death was simply further proof of that.

"We'll keep quiet. It's agreed," Auryn concluded, and we all murmured our assent. Admitting to harbouring a criminal wanted by MI5 was not my idea of smart.

With the gift of hindsight, harbouring a criminal wanted by MI5 seemed like a very bad idea indeed... but things had seemed simple when Joe had been alive. "He was one of the good guys... I was growing more sure of that," I said, before realising I'd spoken aloud.

"His good deeds seem to have landed him in a lot of trouble." Auryn looked sideways at me. "I suppose this is something to do with the animal smuggling?" We'd spent many hours discussing the information Joe had shared with us and his proposed methods for infiltrating the smugglers and shutting down their operation. If truth be told, there hadn't been many developments in the weeks since we'd agreed on a rough plan going forward.

"I don't think it's to do with the smugglers," I said, and then explained my theory as to why it didn't fit. When I'd finished I looked at Tiff's face in the rearview mirror and then across at Auryn. Neither of them looked convinced.

"Obviously it's someone who knows that we know about the smugglers... but I don't think it's one of them," I tried again. "Why would he have been walking around with that document which made me look bad? Who would have known where we kept the ladders? Plus... he was stabbed in the back. That sends a message, too, doesn't it? He betrayed someone."

"He's betrayed a lot of people. It's what criminals do," Auryn muttered. My husband (how strange to think of him as that!) had never seen eye-to-eye with my ex-literary agent. I couldn't say I blamed him for his skepticism, but I genuinely believed that Joe had changed for the better. Or if he hadn't - as far as I could tell - he hadn't managed to see his masterplan through. I decided I would assume the best of him until proved incorrect.

"Hopefully it will all be tidied up soon," Tiff said a little too brightly, considering there had been a murder. She'd hardly been fond of Joe either, but I knew that her false optimism was largely an attempt to salvage the end of the day.

I smiled at her and thanked her for one of the happiest days of my life. Auryn chimed in, echoing my sentiments. Tiff said it was nothing and glowed the rest of the way to the house.

Auryn and I realised we were tired out by our long and eventful day. I handed over my gift and then, in true practical zookeeper style, we went straight to bed, anticipating the early morning.

Auryn fell asleep immediately, but I lay there in the dark, mulling over the murder. My biggest worry was that it meant our little espionage mission was somehow compromised, but I reassured myself that I didn't believe this was to do with the animal smuggling. This attack had felt personal… probably instigated by one of Joe's contacts from his old life, who'd finally caught up with him. The strange legal document that mentioned my old publishing company was surely a testament to that.

I wasn't holding out much hope of the local police force finding his killer, and this was one case I wasn't going to go poking into either. If MI5 couldn't take down Joe's old colleagues, I didn't stand a chance… and they'd already proved themselves capable of murder.

I sighed and shut my eyes, safe in the knowledge that this whole thing would be consigned to the unsolved archives in no time at all. Before I finally drifted off, one thought kept dancing around in my head: You can change everything about your appearance, but it's a lot harder to change the person inside… I frowned at the strange verse, dismissing it as one of those philosophical nonsenses that sometimes haunt us before we sleep. I was too tired to consider that my brain was actually trying to point out something I'd missed.

It was something that meant Joe's death wasn't going to go unnoticed by *them*.

3

THE USUAL SUSPECTS

The next morning we ate wedding cake for breakfast. It was something that we promised ourselves wouldn't become a habit, but Connie Breeze (my chef at The Wild Spot) had outdone herself with such a huge cake I thought we might still be eating it come Christmas.

"Are you ready to go for our first ride as husband and wife?" Auryn asked with such seriousness that I thought something was terribly wrong for a moment. He observed my alarmed expression and grinned. "Just thought I'd set the mood. It's a lovely day. The sun is shining, the autumn leaves are still crisp... they'll cushion you nicely if you fall off."

"Thanks a bunch." I pulled my plate of cake closer and glared at him.

By my side, Rameses whined hopefully, staring at the fruitcake. I shook my head at him and he looked mournfully at me in return. It made me lament not being able to explain how it was bad for dogs and cats to eat fruitcake - communication between humans and animals was surely the greatest challenge there was when it came to animal care. I knew he'd

27

brighten up when we all went out on a hack together, even if the same couldn't be said for his owner.

"I tacked the horses up when you were in the shower. Once you've finished your cake we can go." Auryn was practically bouncing up and down in his chair.

It was only since we'd got the horses that I'd discovered how much he enjoyed riding. I believed that Auryn himself hadn't known it was the case either, until now. He was definitely what people in the right circles would call a born horseman. I'd watched him clear all kinds of hedges, ditches, and fences without batting an eye. When he was on Columbia, he looked every bit as good as the riders you saw competing on TV. I'd spent our first few rides together compiling a hypothesis that I'd been given the troublesome horse, but when Auryn had seen my face-pulling, and had put two and two together, we'd swapped over. I'd been forced to accept the truth: I was the one who was a dud.

"Please, someone save me," I said, lifting my gaze to the heavens while Auryn snorted and shook his head, already in horsey mode.

"Stop being dramatic. We've got that special picnic to take with us, remember? It'll be worth it for the food."

"I knew there was a reason I married you," I told him with a slight smile. Auryn understood me.

Auryn grinned again before opening the fridge and pulling out the pre-packed fancy picnic that had been a rather thoughtful gift from my parents. "Let's get going. We've got organising to do this afternoon."

I found I was smiling more at that thought than the prospect of the morning ride. After much deliberation with Joe, the only thing we'd been able to come up with was an undercover operation. Joe had laughed off our suggestions of a sting, and besides - that would mean risking our own animals in order to pull it off, and we'd essentially be engaging in criminal activity. When everything was uncovered, there was no guarantee that The Lucky Zoo and Avery wouldn't be tarred with the same brush. That was when we'd come up with plan B. While Joe claimed that most of the zoos in the country were implicated in this huge smuggling operation, there were a few big players. One of these big players was only fifty miles away from us, situated close to London. Once we knew that, we'd got to work.

Aside from Joe, who'd reminded us at the time that he wasn't going to join in with any criminal activity - a convenient excuse he'd wheeled out whenever he didn't want to do something - Auryn was the best salesperson among us. He had been the one to approach Corbyn Manor's Zoo Experience with our business pitch.

I'd worked as a consultant, advising zoos on improvements that would help animal welfare and their breeding programmes, for many different zoos. However, Corbyn Manor was larger by far than any I'd worked at before. I'd also never had to tout my services, as clients had always come to me. That was why I'd needed Auryn. If anyone could figure out a way to convince the bigwigs at Corbyn Manor that they needed to employ us, he could.

Auryn went in with a game plan, but he came back out with something even better.

Our real reason for wanting to work at Corbyn Manor was because Joe had informed us that they were responsible for a lot of the animals who were whisked away from British soil and shipped off to unknown, but probably terrible, fates. We knew that to find out the truth, we would have to do so from within. Auryn had hoped to pitch himself as a zoo events consultant and me as an animal welfare and breeding consultant, but apparently our small zoo experience had failed to impress the managers enough to employ us in that role. They had, however, offered us a job... as undercover reviewers. Whilst they'd decided they didn't need any advice on animal care and events (which remained to be seen) they did want a report on how the events they ran and the animals they paid people to look after were really doing. Were the zookeepers doing their jobs correctly? Were the events staff lazy? They wanted us to be their spies.

"Are we double agents?" I'd asked Auryn when he'd told me the job pitch.

"Triple, I think," Auryn had replied, looking bemused. He'd called them back and accepted. Our mission as double or triple agents began first thing tomorrow. It was a strange sort of honeymoon.

The loud thumping at the door snapped me out of my daydream where I was saving animals from smugglers - dressed in a slinky black jumpsuit, for some reason. I blinked and the thumping came again.

"Do you think it's a well-wisher?" I asked as Auryn walked past me with curiosity lining his face.

"Sounds more like trouble," he replied, and I concluded that he was right. Congratulatory calls didn't tend to be accompanied by the sound of someone trying to kick your door down.

"Coming!" Auryn shouted when it was clear that the caller wasn't going to stop hammering. *What if we'd been out?* I wondered. *Would they have carried on until the door had keeled over?*

"Do I know you?" I heard Auryn ask in disgruntled tones. By my side, Rameses growled. I shot him a surprised look before getting up from the kitchen table and going to see who was at the door.

Two figures in dark suits stood on the doorstep, looking like pallbearers at a funeral. My heart dropped what felt like several miles.

"Ms Borel, Mr Flannigan... what can I do for you?" I asked the pair of MI5 vultures.

They turned their sharp eyes on me and I felt every inch of their scrutiny and displeasure.

"We are here to investigate the death of a man wanted by the police. A man we believe was in your employ," Ms Borel said.

I let her words sink in.

My worst fears had been confirmed. MI5 had found out about Joe's death... and they knew as well as I did that he was not your average marketing and PR expert.

"Do you mean Joe Harvey?" I asked, knowing that it was time to play dumb if I wanted to crawl out of the hole they'd already dug for me. "He worked for me doing my zoo's marketing and PR. I wasn't aware that he was in any trouble with the police?" I raised my eyebrows. The pair on the doorstep weren't speaking plainly because of Auryn's presence, but I could already tell from the cloud that had settled over his face that he'd figured out who they were. I hoped that Borel and Flannigan didn't pay him too much attention, or I'd be in even more trouble.

"Due to a lack of contacts for his next of kin and the condition of the body, DNA was taken to aid in formal identification. As soon as it entered the database, we were alerted. Did you know you were employing a man named Rich Summers?" Ms Borel enquired.

I dutifully shook my head, keeping my face studiously blank and hoping that Auryn was doing likewise. I'd assumed that the two identities I'd known Joe by weren't his original given names, but I certainly hadn't imagined him as a Rich Summers. It sounded like the kind of name an American high school sweetheart might possess.

"We believe he also went by the name of Jordan Barnes," Flannigan continued, zeroing in on me.

I'd known it was coming. I geared myself up for what I knew needed to be an Oscar-worthy performance. "Jordan was my literary agent. You know that," I said, frowning in feigned puzzlement. "Have you found him?"

"Yes… he's the man who you found dead last night," Flannigan patiently explained.

I shook my head. "That man was Joe Harvey, my marketing guy. I recognised the shirt he was wearing. I know his face was bad, but… I was sure of it."

"After considering the evidence, we believe the man you are calling Joe Harvey, and your literary agent, are one and the same person." Ms Borel stared so deeply at me I wondered if she could see my bones. "Were you aware of that?"

I shook my head, hoping to imply muteness caused by the shock revelation.

The looks on their faces more than hinted that they didn't believe me for a second. So much for a career in acting!

"I don't understand why he wasn't identified as Joe Harvey? I told the police that was who he was. I always do background checks on all of my employees. He had all of the right paperwork. Birth certificate… driver's license… next of kin…" He'd had it all. I'd asked for it in order to be difficult, due to my initial reluctance to employ him.

To employ a member of staff, I needed certain details, but I'd made it even tougher in Joe's case. He'd handed it all over with glee and (although I'd assumed they had to be fakes) they'd looked like the real deal. Even his next of kin contact had checked out. I was certain that in the case of Joe Harvey's death, he wouldn't have neglected to leave a proper paper trail that reassured whomever found him that he was who he was currently claiming to be, thus making a DNA test unnecessary. The only spanner in the works was the killer's deliberate attack on his face.

Someone had wanted him to be identified using DNA.

Then, there was his strange death to consider and the facts that didn't add up. The ladder... the knife in the back... and the ruination of his face, necessitating the DNA test which had revealed his true identity. I'd already suspected that Joe's murderer had prior knowledge of who he was, but now I was certain that something fishy was going on. Could this whole thing have been some sort of a set-up? I didn't trust any of these people an inch, and I was alarmed by the prospect of their sudden re-entry into my life.

"Ms Amos... I think you knew who you were employing," Flannigan said.

I surveyed the skeptical man in front of me, realising that I'd never really taken the time to actually look at him properly. His hair was a pleasant brown and starting to thin on the top. He was older than thirty, but younger than fifty. His eyes were nearly colourless. And that was all there was to say about Mr Flannigan. He was completely nondescript. He was the perfect spy.

"Mrs," I corrected. I'd been wondering if I'd remember to make that little change, but when faced with a couple of characters I would do everything I could to be difficult with, it came like instinct.

Flannigan's eyebrows might have raised as much as a centimetre as he beheld the rings on my fingers and looked across at the man by my side. I was reminded that in a different life, this strange, slinking man had expressed his own interest in me. Even now it made me shudder.

"I had no idea who he really was," I told him flatly, and that - as far as I was concerned - was an end to it.

To my surprise, the agents seemed to agree. With one further unreadable look exchanged between them, they wrapped things up.

"We'll be investigating this crime for some time to come. Can we rely on your co-operation?" Ms Borel enquired.

"Of course. I'll let the zoo staff know to give you any access you need," I said, figuring that if I appeared amenable in some respects, they might believe I was being as helpful as I could be in all areas. I nearly added that they already knew their way around the place, so could make themselves at home, but I remembered in the nick of time that Auryn was standing next to me... supposedly oblivious to the murky undercurrents.

I remained looking out through the glass in the front door even after they'd turned and walked back up the long drive. When I'd found Joe's body in the lynx enclosure, my first thought had been that it meant trouble. There'd been too many little things wrong with the scene that had been presented to me. MI5 turning up on my doorstep proved as much, but it didn't answer the question I had in my mind... the answer to which I believed would lead me straight to the killer.

Who else had guessed Joe Harvey's true identity?

In spite of the unwelcome visitors, our ride through the countryside was actually rather enjoyable. The autumn leaves swirled to the ground as we cantered past, and Smokey only nearly threw me off once when Auryn decided to jump a log and she wilfully followed Columbia's lead. My new husband had laughed when he'd spotted me clinging to the horse's neck and had expressed his amusement that, while I professed to know so much about caring for animals, I sure as heck couldn't ride one. I'd then accused him of not being very encouraging and had threatened to walk the rest of the way. It wasn't long after that when we'd decided to stop for our picnic, and quarrelsome words were forgotten in the face of good food.

"Do you think they're going to let us get away?" Auryn asked once we'd finished the autumnal spiced apple pie that had been packed in the lunch.

"What happened to Joe is terrible, but... it's not the biggest shock in the world, is it?" I said, knowing that Auryn would understand that I wasn't being callous, just realistic. I'd always liked my ex-literary agent, even though he'd liked to try my patience at times. Since he'd been working for me, I'd grown even closer to him and had begun thinking of him as one of the good guys. Perhaps I was a fool for believing him, that remained to be seen, but I would certainly miss him.

"I don't like those people just turning up and demanding answers."

I shook my head. I didn't like it much either. "I always wondered if they would come back. I was warned that once you know the truth it's hard to get away from it."

"We should just let them get on with it. We've got our own investigation to conduct." There was a brief pause before Auryn continued. "We can do our bit for Joe that way," he said, making an effort to be decent.

I smiled at him. "We'd better make sure we do a good job."

There was the sound of sweet chestnuts falling from the trees and the scent of autumn rose up around us as we sat on our rug in the cool, but pleasant, sunshine. It was a moment of peace in a life of happy madness and I drank it in as deeply as I could.

A moment later, my phone rang. I mouthed 'sorry' at Auryn and answered it, feeling reality return with a bump.

"Hi Katya," I said, greeting my only friend in British Intelligence.

She didn't return my greeting.

"Your animal smuggling source was one of our most wanted men, and you didn't think to tell me? In fact... you were employing him? I can't believe you!" I could hear the deep hurt in her voice. "And don't claim that you didn't know who he really was. You're smart, Madi. You can tell the bosses whatever you like, but I know the truth. A lot of my career has been tied up with these money launderers, and all this time you knew how to find them."

"I don't know anything about money launderers," I said, keeping my voice kind. I could see her point, and heck - I'd been torn up over the very same thing when Joe had admitted his true identity, only to buy my silence with the knowledge and contacts needed to take down the animal smuggling group. Now he was dead and I had to assume that all of his usefulness had died with him. Should I really remain loyal to a man who'd basically bribed his way into my good graces? "We're still going ahead with the plan to infiltrate the zoo, but I understand if you're busy..."

"I am busy. I think I might be busy forever," Katya said shortly.

I silently sighed. "I'm sorry," I said before ending the call.

"What's wrong?" Auryn asked, taking a break from gathering chestnuts and seeing my miserable expression.

"I think I just lost a friend," I confessed. Sadly, I didn't have that many to lose.

"I can see why Katya would be upset," Auryn agreed, pulling the same troubled expression I knew was on my own face. "You were between a rock and a hard place. Joe deliberately made it that way. He played on your feelings, knowing that you'd want to save animals above all else."

"But I went along with it... even though we have nothing to show for it. It could all be lies," I fretted, wondering if I'd been fed a line from the start. Had it all been a source of amusement for Joe?

"I don't think it's a lie. Look at the way that zoo failed to explain Liberty's existence. Look inside yourself and ask your gut. Mine tells me that the smuggling is real and that there's rot eating away at the heart of many of the zoos in this country."

I nodded, feeling the same truth in my bones. We didn't have irrefutable evidence and, aside from Liberty, a lot was taken on faith, but that had been the whole point of the mission we were going on - to gather proof.

"But I did keep quiet about a criminal's identity. They're supposed to fund all sorts of awful things... terrorism... gun smuggling. It's all bad. Joe claimed that it was only one side of the story, but I don't know. He's been murdered. We might already be in deeper than we know, and the problem is, we actually know so little," I fretted.

"We'll just have to keep trying. But we should also be careful. Our only contact with the criminal underworld has been killed and, as yet, we don't know why."

We sat in gloomy silence for a moment, both contemplating everything that lay before us. *And now we've lost Katya as well*, I silently added.

"We've got to do it on our own," Auryn said, reaching a final verdict at the same time I did. At the end of the day, this wasn't about us. Sure, we had it relatively easy with our successful zoos and my comics, but could we truly enjoy it all if we knew that there was massive animal abuse going on right under our noses and we could have had the chance to stop it? I doubted it very much.

"Let's get back and prepare," I said.

We were close to being ready to leave for our new jobs the next morning when there was a knock on the door. It wasn't quite so ferocious a knock as when Ms Borel and Mr Flannigan had come to call, but the early hour still made us exchange alarmed looks.

With much trepidation, we walked down the hall to answer it together.

"Lowell?!" I said, horrified to see my ex-boyfriend standing on the doorstep. In my shock at seeing him there, I'd forgotten that his real name was actually Luke, but that was all well and good considering the presence of Auryn, who was supposed to be clueless and know Lowell by his 'private detective' name.

"What are you doing here?" my husband growled at the man on the doorstep. Regardless of Lowell's true mission, Auryn was well-entitled to know that the visitor had hurt me badly.

"I'm working," Lowell said with an apology written across his face.

"Why would the police employ a private detective?" Auryn asked, crossing his arms with skepticism evident in his voice. I glanced across at him and reflected that Lowell would have to be a fool to not work out that Auryn knew something of the truth.

"It's a complicated matter. I am officially employed to work with them." He flashed us an ID that I assumed was genuine. MI5 could obtain whatever they wanted in terms of security clearance.

"What are you doing here?" I repeated, unsatisfied with his first answer.

Lowell pushed past into the house without invitation. "I'm here to check your post. It hasn't come yet, has it?"

I shook my head, not taking my eyes off the man I'd rejected when I'd discovered he was keeping secrets from me. Later, I'd learned he'd actually been thrust into my path with the intention of infiltrating the money laundering group, using my comic as bait. He looked back at me with his dark eyes and I thought I saw a flash of regret for a moment, but I'd learned long ago not to trust Lowell.

"Post should be here in half an hour or so. Knock yourself out," I told him, before turning around and walking back upstairs to my office to continue gathering supplies for our imminent trip.

I hoped the post-lady would be on time this morning. I didn't want to leave Lowell in the house, but I also didn't want us to be late on our first day. Telling an employer that you were delayed due to your post being searched for evidence in a murder investigation was hardly going to do our undercover mission any favours. If the zoo really did have criminal contacts, they might even find out who the people sniffing around Joe's murder really were.

Why does he even need to look through our post? I wondered and a light frown took up residence on my forehead. Did they think that Joe had conveniently sent me a letter detailing how to find his old gang of money launderers? *Perhaps he has,* I thought, remembering that he'd managed to send through legal documents that dissolved my publishing contract, even as he was on the run from the authorities. While he'd got away with it that time, it was clear that his methods hadn't gone unnoticed by MI5. I wondered how they'd found out about it and could only assume that they'd discovered a courier had been sent to my house during their post-investigation research, as they scrambled to find out what had gone wrong.

The bright ring of the doorbell startled me. With two sets of people intent on battering down the door, I'd forgotten we had a fully functioning doorbell.

To my annoyance, I walked down the stairs to discover Lowell had already answered the door and was rifling through my post in front of a baffled post lady. I waved to show that this rude man was grudgingly permitted to raid our post and she hurried off, eager to be away. I couldn't say I blamed her.

Lowell's attention was focused on the parcel she'd rung the doorbell to deliver. He held it away from his body and gingerly turned it this way and that... as if expecting it to blow up.

"Is it a bomb?" I asked sarcastically from my relatively safe place on the stairs.

"I doubt it," Lowell replied, deadly serious. "It's addressed to you. It looks like the same stationary that was used in the last delivery you received. I think this is what we're looking for." He tucked the parcel under his arm and made to walk out of the still-open door.

"Hey! You're not even going to open it? It's my post! I should get to see what's inside." I knew there was a serious investigation going on, but I still thought it was pretty rude to mindlessly confiscate my post without first knowing the contents.

"You'll probably be informed and questioned about the contents once it has been analysed," Lowell said in a horribly formal fashion. His dark eyes regarded me for a moment and I tried not to think about the time we'd spent together. I was happily married to Auryn, but being faced with Lowell gave me this horrible wrenching feeling inside. I knew that it was regret.

"Fine," I said, giving in. I'd mentally weighed up the desire to know what was inside the parcel against my desire to get rid of Lowell and had reached a very definite conclusion. MI5 could have whatever they wanted, so long as I didn't have to spend any time with him.

I shut the door behind my traitorous ex-boyfriend and bent down to gather up the rest of the post. In my mind, I whispered an apology to Joe that whatever final communication he'd sent to me hadn't got through. I considered all that I'd known about the man and concluded that if he'd thought the authorities would be onto him so quickly in the event of his death, he wouldn't have used the same method of post-disaster communication. Now I may never find out what he'd sent me.

I flipped through the rest of the post, finding bills and junk for the most part. There was a thank you note for being invited to the wedding, which touched me a lot, and then there was another handwritten envelope. I opened it, thinking it would probably be another well-wisher congratulating us on our marriage.

It turned out to be a death threat.

4

BURROWS AND BURIED SKELETONS

My first thought was that it was a terrible cliché. Someone had spent a lot of time strenuously cutting letters out of newspapers and magazines. He or she had then glued them onto this piece of paper. It was even missing a few letters where the glue the person had used hadn't been good enough, but I still got the message:

If you talk to the cops, you die.

Talk about what?! I wondered, completely baffled by this strange death threat. I called Auryn and showed him the letter, before instinctively going to call the police. I hesitated before dialling. Did the letter mean I wasn't supposed to tell the police about the death threat? It was all so confusing. In the end, I dialled Katya's number and prayed she'd pick up.

"What?" my ex-friend barked into the receiver.

I explained I'd received a death threat in the post warning me to not talk to the police and that Lowell had missed it.

"What an idiot," Katya said. I hoped she was referring to Lowell and not me. "Someone will come over in a few minutes to get it." There was a little pause and then she added: "Be safe," before hanging up.

In spite of the death threat I felt a small smile lift my cheeks. Perhaps there was hope for repairing our friendship after all.

Our first day on the new job turned out to be nothing of the sort. We arrived, only for the woman we were meeting with to hustle us in through the back door. At first, Auryn and I had exchanged panicked glances, worried that somehow we'd already been compromised. The real reason for our secretive entrance was soon revealed when the woman berated us without even introducing herself.

"You do know you're supposed to be here undercover, don't you?" She looked at me with thinly-veiled disgust.

"Oh... I'm famous," I said, frowning a little as I tried to remember. Living in Gigglesfield in splendid isolation, I never found my fame to be too troublesome. I knew that my publishing company still liked to use my face and story to promote my comics, but I supposed I'd sort of hoped I'd slipped off the radar - in spite of the TV appearances and press conferences that cropped up quite regularly. Again, I'd kind of considered them to be a different life from mine... it was something that happened to someone else - not the woman who owned the zoo.

"Yes, you are. I was sent here to meet you and show you around, but I can see that would be completely stupid - unless we want to tip everyone off as to who you are.

43

Everyone knows you were a zookeeper turned animal consultant. They'll know in a second that you're here to check up on them."

"Right," I said, nodding in agreement and wondering how we could have been so foolish not to realise. I supposed it was probably due to the wedding and the terrible event that had followed it. Everything still felt surreal. It was a stark reminder that Auryn and I should really be on our guard if we wanted to uncover the animal abusers and escape without being caught ourselves.

"So, it's agreed. You'll come back here tomorrow with a disguise so good, I'll struggle to recognise you," the woman announced, already walking us back towards the entrance we'd come through.

"Sorry… who are you?" Auryn asked before we were booted back outside.

"Jennifer Bucket. I'm one of the executives here. I've been given the responsibility of handling your assignment. Back here at nine in the morning tomorrow," she said and promptly shut the door in our faces.

"Was that efficiency or rudeness?" Auryn asked.

I shrugged back at him, equally unsure. "Perhaps that's the way things are done at large zoos."

Auryn grunted his disapproval. "No wonder they're rotten at their core if that's the way they treat their staff."

On that ominous note, we returned home to work on our disguises. Little did we know, they'd come in handy sooner than our return to the zoo.

We were up bright and early the next morning, turning the horses out in the garden, when we saw the intruder. Rameses noticed him at the same time and broke off from playing with the two full-grown foxes who liked to hang around our house from time to time. He ran towards the shadowy figure who'd just scaled the wall by the side of our house, barking an enthusiastic greeting.

A purebred Pharaoh Hound, Rameses is not the largest dog ever, but I could certainly see why someone who didn't know his soft nature would scramble back up the way they came.

"Was that a burglar?" Auryn muttered, as mystified as I was.

Together, we walked back to the house to see if we could find any evidence that we were being broken-in to.

As soon as I walked into the front room, the window lit up as flashes went off. I was forced to retreat back into the hall to regain my eyesight. Then the shouting began.

"Madi! Is it true you received a death threat?"

"Was the man found murdered in the lynx enclosure really working for you?"

"Was he blackmailing you over the rights to your comics?"

I felt more confused by the second as the shouts continued, until finally…

"What made you murder one of your employees and feed him to the lynx?"

I made a sound of utter disbelief and walked away from the press hounds. Auryn stood next to me in the kitchen with an ashen face, having heard the same set of accusations.

"I always knew they'd turn on me one day," I said.

"How do they know all of that stuff? It's supposed to be a secret investigation, isn't it? I mean, for goodness' sake, *they're* involved. You'd think there'd be a blanket ban on any information getting out. It was only this morning they reported that death threat. Do you think it's been released to the public?" He pushed a hand back through his blonde hair, looking older than his years when trouble lined his face.

"I doubt that. I think someone has got a big mouth." I was thinking about the money launderers' miraculous last-minute escape from the clutches of MI5 when I said it. Back then, it had been suspected that someone who was in on the highly exclusive operation had let the cat out of the bag. To my knowledge, the leak had never been found. It would appear that they were at it again.

"Why would they accuse you of killing Joe? You couldn't have possibly done it. We were getting married!"

I nodded emphatically. "They just want a story. Good thing we'll be out of the local area as of this morning." The thought of us sneaking out in our disguises under the noses of the press now seemed amusing. At the very least, it would be a good chance to test them out.

"I'm glad we're going. I hate to add another theory, but what if they have deliberately let this information slip to the press? They know we're not being completely straight with them. What if they really do believe you know more about the money launderers than you're letting on? If the press go after you believing that you're involved with it and make you out to be some kind of criminal, perhaps they're hoping that the launderers will come out of the woodwork." I noted that he didn't specify whether they'd be coming to save me or get rid of me. I think we both knew which was more likely. "It could all be a set-up."

I turned and looked down the corridor towards where I knew the baying press waited outside, hoping for a good story to slap on the front page. A story that the entire country would know about. The phrase 'set-up' seemed to be echoing around in my head a lot.

"You may be right," I said, thinking dark thoughts about the value MI5 put on their investigations, versus a person's safety. They wanted their launderers, and I was to be the sacrificial lamb.

My phone rang a few minutes after we'd decided that we'd better get into our disguises and sneak out down the garden, if we were to be on time. It was then agreed that Auryn would go back alone (being less likely to be recognised) and collect the car, before the press got wind of what was happening.

"Hi Gloria," I said, seeing my publisher's name flash up on screen.

"Is it true that the validity of our contract has been called into question?" She sounded hurt and angry.

"Not to my knowledge," I immediately replied, sparing a thought to be impressed with just how quickly word could spread. "My contract with Rock and Roll Publishing was officially dissolved prior to their mysterious disappearance." It had actually been afterwards, but I didn't wish to muddy the waters further. "I have the paperwork, but you checked it yourself when you signed me," I gently reminded her.

Gloria sniffed. "Yes, well... I suppose you're right. It was all in order..." Now she sounded apologetic. "You just hear things. I wasn't sure what to believe."

You and me both, I privately thought.

"No harm done. I'm sure you already know, but one of my employees was murdered yesterday. He had on his person something that I believe was planted to incriminate me." I was growing surer of that by the second. The inexplicable leaking of the information to the press only confirmed it in my mind. Someone wanted suspicion to fall upon me. Someone who was playing us all for fools.

"It was brought to my attention. I'm sorry I didn't ask you first. I only hope the press don't stick with this line for too long..."

I should have known that Gloria Lenin's mind would

turn back to business before long. She was a lovely woman, but she was also very good at her job, and her job was to sell books.

"I hope they don't either. I had nothing to do with Joe's death."

"It does seem terribly unfair. I don't mean to sound callous, but it could be a major blow for your career if this tarnishes your reputation."

I found I appreciated Gloria cutting to the chase. It was harsh for sure, but she was only telling the hard truth. This could spell trouble for *Monday's Menagerie*. In the past, I'd probably have shrugged it off. Easy come, easy go. It was only ever supposed to be a hobby, but I'd grown to enjoy my comic's success. It made people happy, and I liked having the ability to do that. I didn't want to disappoint the public by not being the person the press had originally made me out to be. I was no saint, but I certainly wasn't a killer.

"I'm sure this will all blow over. The press can be so silly at times," Gloria said in a reassuring tone that I didn't buy. She was better at telling hard truths than sharing words of false comfort.

"It will be sorted," I told her in a voice I knew was filled with steel. Someone involved in this investigation had a lot to answer for, and I was making it my mission to find out who.

"We'd better go," Auryn interjected, miming pointing at a watch.

I threw my hands up in the air in frustration, before tearing up the stairs and applying my disguise. When that was done, I spared a moment to examine myself in the mirror.

It didn't look quite as good as it had done yesterday afternoon when I'd tried the 'new me' on for the first time, but I thought it would probably do the job. I'd purchased a lovely gently curling auburn wig which only itched a little. My makeup had been done to the best of my memory along the lines that the makeup artist had done it when I was supposed to have gone on camera with TV personality, Ben Ravenwood. The final touch had been to trade my glasses for contact lenses. I'd always hated putting things in my eyes, but I'd been forced to agree that it was something that changed my appearance beyond recognition. Now the only giveaway could be my small stature. We'd thought about changing that with platform shoes, but I'd remembered that we were both working undercover roles suited to our infiltration tasks... and I was hardly going to do a great job as a zookeeper if I was tottering around in high heels all day.

"This is weird," Auryn said, looking at me in a way that let me know he preferred the normal, non-made-up me. Auryn's own disguise took some getting used to. Instead of messing around with wigs and such, he'd gone to the barbers yesterday and got himself an average-Joe haircut. His surfer-style locks were gone. Instead, he wore his hair short on the sides and longer on top in a style that eerily resembled Lowell's. Unfortunately, the colour was a little close to Lowell's for comfort, too. Auryn had chosen to dye it semi-permanently darker. Hair dye had been as far as Auryn had felt he needed to go, due to his not being nearly so famous, but it was still a big change. I felt my own expression mirror that of my husband's.

"We're still us," I said with a half smile.

"It'll wash out in no time. I quite like it short though," Auryn confessed, checking himself out in the bedroom mirror.

"Stop preening. We need to go!"

Five minutes later, we were in the woods handing over Rameses and our back door keys to a bemused Tiff, who'd agreed to take Rameses to the zoo with her and pop back and feed the animals if we were late returning.

"I doubt I'd have known you if you walked past me on the street," Tiff said taking in my appearance. "Look how pretty you are with makeup." She bit her lip. "But I think I prefer you the way you are normally."

"Less competition, eh?" I joked. It would be tough for a supermodel to compete with Tiff.

She waved a self-deprecating hand in my direction. "You look great no matter what you do, Madi. Well... apart from when you've been chasing the feral cats through the hedges."

I glared at her for a second. Since I'd left Avery Zoo, Tiff had taken on the care of the feral cats who lived in a barn outside of Avery Zoo and kept the rodent population down. However, I'd been a little too close to home during this year's 'kitten season'. We did our best to make sure every cat of the right age was neutered, but new cats were always arriving and often gave birth to new litters of kittens, who in turn needed neutering to stem the unending tide of cats. Our goals were not to wipe out feral cats, but merely to ensure they had healthy, happy, and long lives. There were always new cats coming our way, and those few who managed to slip the net meant there were always going to be kittens.

The hardest part of neutering the feral cats was catching them. If you were lucky, you could bait a trap and miraculously catch the right cat. But what usually happened was you caught the lazy old tom who doesn't like to hunt but enjoys a free meal. Then you have to move onto plan B, which involves a lot of tearing around with a large butterfly net... and, as Tiff had mentioned, running through hedges.

"Has Alex found anything out about the murder?" I asked Tiff, unable to keep the question inside. I knew it was bad for her to gossip about police business, but then... someone already had, hadn't they?

Tiff shook her head. "The police seem to be stalling out. Because there's all of this suspicion about Joe being a wanted fugitive…" She made air quotations with her fingers when she said that. Tiff knew the truth as well as Auryn did. "…it means that the little old local police don't get a look in. For all intents and purposes, Alex is off the case and back looking for lost cats and stolen purses."

"Would he have known that I received a death threat yesterday?" I asked.

Tiff's gaze sharpened for a moment. "I'm not sure. He never mentioned it." She took the keys from Auryn and wished us a good first day of work, before walking off through the woods in the opposite direction.

"Way to put your foot in it," Auryn said, not unkindly. I'd told him what I'd been told about Alex Gregory's true identity. He'd agreed that it was a tough decision as to whether or not to tell Tiff. We only had one man's word and a healthy amount of suspicion that the detective was quite possibly not everything he appeared to be. My friend had just married the man, and we didn't want to ruin anything before we were absolutely sure about Alex Gregory. I still had everything crossed that we were wrong.

"You think she suspects we suspect something?" Tiff was no dummy and I was worried that - as ever - my face was an open book.

"Perhaps it's more that she suspects something herself," Auryn finished, sounding grim. "I hope that everything works out okay. I want Tiff to have a happy family," he said, referring to Tiff's unborn child.

"So do I," I echoed, meaning every word.

If Alex Gregory was working for anyone other than the police force, the press' claim that I was a killer could prove to be true.

Jennifer Bucket looked marginally happier to see us this morning. Our disguises got a single nod of approval before we were hustled beyond the first doorway and into a room containing various Corbyn Manor's Zoo Experience uniforms. We'd both known our general roles prior to this moment, but it was now that Jennifer revealed the exact nature of the phoney jobs they'd rustled up for us.

"Madigan, you will be joining our resident pet's corner keeper to help her with our recent expansion of the pet zone. I'm sure she'll be glad to have a keeper with your experience at her side."

I nodded. We'd discussed it with the executives when Auryn and I had been called in for an interview/job pitch. It had been agreed that I could share the experience I'd gained from working at other zoos, but not reveal too many specifics about locations that could lead anyone to suspect my real identity.

"Auryn, I'm afraid the only event staff we recruit at this time of year are seasonal Halloween staff, who mostly work entertaining the children. It's not a high-level job, but you'll get a good view of what we do from the ground level up… and I'm sure you'll have the perfect perspective on how managers and staff members alike work and are treated." She gave him a slightly apologetic shrug. I could tell that Auryn was being handed a pig of a job, and would no doubt learn exactly how the managers treated their underlings as he would be on the bottom of the pile. I was sure it would make for an interesting report, but probably not a fun time for Auryn.

My husband winced. "Oh well… I've been the dogsbody before." His usual grin was back in place a second later, and I knew he was reminiscing about his time spent at Avery working as an apprentice zookeeper.

I kept my smile to myself. Auryn may think he had real-world bottom-of-the-pile job experience, but he'd always been a privileged member of Avery Zoo due to his parentage. I thought that this would be an interesting dose of reality.

However, I wasn't too smug about my own position. I hated petting zoos with a passion. They were so often places of animal cruelty where children were allowed to run rampant and animals were left uncared for. I decided to look on the bright side. No matter how bad the situation might be, I would hopefully be able to do something to make it better. Auryn and I may be at the zoo under false pretences, but I still wanted us to do a great job. Until we figured out what was going on and who was responsible, I wanted to believe that there were still a lot of people who cared about making Corbyn Manor a better zoo.

"Good luck, Aaron," I said to Auryn, using the name we'd concocted as cover.

"Good luck, Molly," he said in return, barely able to suppress his laugh.

Names like ours could be a blessing and a curse. With the way things were regarding social media and the internet, neither of us could risk one of our new colleagues searching for us online, and you'd have to be living under a rock to have not at least heard a whisper of my name when working in the zoo business. Instead, we'd picked easy to remember names, starting with the same letter of our own names, and we were both claiming a deep suspicion of all things internet related - which was why there was absolutely no trace of us online. Suspicious it may be, but it was better than anyone knowing the truth.

I nodded one more time at Auryn, still weirded out by his new hair. Then I went to uncover the truth.

"Hi," I said, walking into the room I'd been told was the keeper-specific staffroom. No one much turned round. I was met with a sea of heads. Everyone was holding cups of coffee and various coffee break snacks. Was everyone here a zookeeper? A look at their uniforms confirmed it. There were so many of them!

"Where have you come from?" a man asked. His smile had something predatory about it. I felt like I was being examined by a shark.

"I'm new here. I've worked at a few other zoos, but nowhere as big as this place."

"I can tell," the man continued, still watching me in that strange way I didn't like. "Where in particular?"

"Snidely Safari and Pendalay Zoo," I said without missing a beat. I'd messaged both zoos about my undercover mission (the Corbyn approved version) and they'd agreed to back me up if anyone enquired about a Molly Adley. "I'm supposed to be working with Robyn," I said, remembering the name of the pet zone keeper.

An expression of boredom immediately took over the creepy man's features. "She's over there." He jerked a thumb in the direction of the coffee machine, keeping his beady black eyes fixed on me.

"Which animals do you work with?" I asked, unable to put my finger on this man.

"Amphibians," he said with a wide grin.

Well, that figured.

I tried to keep a friendly smile on my face as I turned away from the creepy keeper and walked over to where he'd motioned my new partner in crime was.

"Hi, are any of you Robyn?" I asked when I arrived at the coffee machine.

Two waif-like women and an older, but very well turned out, lady, regarded me like I'd just told them I'd stepped in tiger poo. They parted like the sea and all looked towards the table on the other side of the coffee machine, where a woman was busy putting away doughnuts like there was no tomorrow.

"Are you Robyn?" I asked as she demolished one with pink icing.

"You betcha I am! Would you be my new buddy?" She had a twinkle in her eye and icing sugar on her left cheek. I decided right there and then that I liked her.

"I hope so! I'm Molly," I said, offering my hand. She brushed it aside and pulled me in for a slightly sticky hug.

"Doughnut? There are still some really good ones left. Try this one, it's filled with caramel cream." She picked up a chocolate covered doughnut and placed it in my hand. I couldn't hide my grin as I bit into the doughnut, well aware of the horrified glances being shot in our direction, courtesy of the guardians of the coffee machine.

"This is awesome," I told her after a heavenly mouthful. "Hey, would you mind letting me know who everyone is? I've only worked at small places before and this is pretty over-whelming."

"Don't you worry about it. You'll get to know everyone in time! The good and the bad. But I'll be your road map. You're going to love it here!"

I picked up on the little phrase she'd inserted in-between all of the warm and fuzzies. "Are there some keepers worth avoiding?" I might have subtly looked towards the coffee machine when I said it.

Robyn looked uncomfortable for a moment. "It's like any workplace, really. You don't always get along with everyone. But you seem like a really nice gal. I'm sure everyone will like you."

"Thanks," I said, thinking that her sentiment certainly wouldn't hold true if anyone found out what I was really doing here.

"Okey-dokey! I think I'm all doughnut-ed out for the day. D'you wanna go and meet the critters?" She had a big grin plastered on her face, but I noticed it falter for a moment when the three women at the coffee machine sniggered.

I glared at them, already drawing up battle lines. It alarmed me that I'd spotted sure signs of bullying just moments after being introduced to the keeper I was working with. Theoretically, I was only supposed to be here to report on animal welfare and how the keepers worked, but I was certainly going to condemn anyone who was bullying another keeper. It would never have happened at a smaller zoo. If anyone tried it, they would soon be put right by the rest of the team, because that's what small zoos were - a team.

We strolled through the zoo with Robyn making observations about the animals and chatting about who was in charge of looking after them. Her blonde ponytail bounced up and down and the smile never slipped from her round cheeks.

"There the lemurs are. Aren't they cute? The primate keepers here are okay. That's Tony, Jill, Winnie, and George. They always say hi to you in the mornings." We continued our walk past the big cats and Robyn's smile wobbled a little. "You already met one of the big cat keepers, Rosa. The woman with the shiny dark hair at the coffee machine? She looks after the leopards and panthers and the cheetahs. She works with Harry and Lee. They do a great job with their animals," Robyn finished after searching for a compliment for a few moments. I realised that Robyn really didn't like to speak ill of anyone, no matter how nasty I presumed they were to her.

"Look at those alligators, eh? Once, we had a child fall into the enclosure. That was scary, I tell you! Fortunately, Rowena, the keeper who looks after the smaller amphibians and reptiles, was on hand. She got right in there and saved him before the gators got too close."

"What about the alligator keeper?"

Robyn looked uncomfortable for another second. "That would be Kel. He was there, too. I think he musta frozen up, or something. It happens you know." She nodded reassuringly, but I was getting a different picture.

"I think I met Kel this morning," I said and described the keeper I'd first made contact with when I'd entered the staffroom.

"Uh-huh, that sounds like him. Just ignore him if he asks you any questions about the rabbit overpopulation problem," Robyn said and then breezed on to chatting about the parrots like nothing had ever happened.

I thought I could figure out exactly why Kel would be interested in the rabbits, and it wasn't to keep as pets.

"We're nearly here! The parrots are kind of on the border of our territory. Sometimes they come into the pet zone to educate visitors, you know? But we never take the birds of prey in! That would cause bedlam. One time, they were flying an eagle. It went off course and swooped right over here. You never heard such a commotion in your life! They fly them a lot further away now."

We turned the corner and were met with a large wooden archway. The sign at the top read 'The Pet Zone' in rainbow coloured letters. I immediately felt a wash of dread at the overall cheeriness of it all, but I hid my feelings with a smile.

"Come on! I'll introduce you to the inmates before it gets too busy. Half-term is on its way and we've got a lot to be preparing for."

Robyn bounced up to the first enclosure on the left. "This

here is our pygmy goat enclosure. Well… what's supposed to be our pygmy enclosure anyhow. You might notice we've got some bigger ones in here. They don't bother the pygmies, but they do help in fending off the older children who get too boisterous with the little ones! These goats look out for each other."

In my experience, big, mean goats picked on whoever was an easy target, but that remained to be seen. "Do the visitors feed them?" I asked, dreading the answer.

"Yes indeedy! They all get a little pack of plain popcorn when they go in. However, there's a cap on the amount they all get a day. We've had weight problems with some of the greedy ones and the cap seems to be helping. The other thing we've done is to move the real chubsters into one of the closed pens, in with the donkeys, so that they can get healthy again… and also learn a few manners. They don't put up with any nonsense!" She winced a little when she said it. "You'll understand when you meet our donkeys." She walked to the right and pointed at the fence, which was awash with notices telling people to not feed the donkeys and to definitely not try to touch them. "None of it works. Bitten fingers are just par for the course here!"

She led on, introducing me to the Indian Runner duck flock, the miniature pigs, the Shetland ponies, the friendly sheep, the ferrets, the chickens, the gerbils, the rats and mice, and finally, the rabbits.

"These little guys are my favourite," Robyn said, climbing over into the enclosure. She was immediately surrounded by several whiffling noses. "Oh, you guys…" she said, pulling a carrot out of her pocket and breaking it into bits. "I swear it's an occasional treat," she told me, but I thought Robyn might have just told her first porky pie.

"There are so many of them," I remarked, looking out

across the green, hilly (and hole-ey) landscape at bunnies of all different sizes.

"That's actually where I'm hoping you can help. I was told you're a breeding expert. Do you think you might be able to figure out how to make these guys stop?!"

"Haven't you…" I mimed snipping motions in the air with my fingers.

Robyn nodded enthusiastically. "We've done the boys and the girls. It's good for them you know. Helps them live longer. But we still get litters appearing, as if from nowhere. It's a real mystery. I thought maybe there were so many rabbits we missed a few, but I don't think that's it. It just keeps happening."

I walked around the enclosure, nodding as I listened to her explanation. It didn't take me long to find what I was looking for. There was a divot of turf that looked out of place. When I prodded at it, it gave way, revealing a hole.

"Do you know the exact number of rabbits you have here?" I asked, sensing I may have already solved the mystery.

Robyn came and stood by me, looking down at the hole. "You know, that's the funny thing. It keeps changing."

"I think you might have some going out and some coming back in. Wild rabbits can and will breed with domesticated European rabbits, if given the chance. If we walk out of the zoo into those fields, we'll probably find the beginnings of a feral and wild colony. They come back in to nest and give birth because the conditions are preferable. Nice food, no predators. Who can blame them?"

Robyn shook her head in wonder. "That would explain a lot! We've had plenty of smaller rabbits with more common brown colouration being born. They're also not the friend-liest, if truth be told."

I nodded. There was a big difference between wild rabbits

and domestic rabbits that had been bred for their friendliness. Even if you rescued a wild rabbit as a kitten, there was still a very good chance that it wouldn't like or trust humans.

"I guess we should block up that hole," Robyn was saying.

"They'll probably dig another one." I paused to think about it. "You'll need to add more rabbit proofing both to the interior and the exterior of the enclosure. Perhaps some natural deterrents on the outside, too. It's easy to make a homemade repellent that won't harm the rabbits or other animals, but it should keep them away." I knew that because Tiff had experienced a rabbit problem at her old rented accommodation. The problem hadn't so much been the rabbits, but what they did to her rescued dogs. They went mad when they saw little bunnies popping up in the garden, and Tiff also didn't like to think of them potentially being mangled by her pets. Soft-hearted Tiff had experimented with a homemade repellant using chilli powder, garlic, and dish soap, spraying it on the rabbits' favourite grazing patches. It had worked a treat and the rabbits had relocated.

"I think you mean *we'll* need to do all that. We're a team now, partner!" She beamed at me. "What about the rabbits who've been born recently? They won't ever get really friendly if they're half wild, will they?"

I shrugged. "You never know. They're not fully wild. I'm sure some of them will be just as friendly as any rabbit." I privately thought that it was no bad thing if the resident rabbits had an inbuilt sense of self-preservation. They would probably need it when faced with hordes of grabby kids.

"You sure know a lot about rabbits. I reckon you'll fit right in here in the pet zone. You probably already know we're expanding. That's why they finally let me have a buddy!"

I tried to do my best to look well-informed. As my job role wasn't genuine, I could only assume that they'd thought

I could make things up as I went along. "This is going to sound silly, but in the rush of the interviews, I think I was too overwhelmed to take much in. It was just too exciting." I felt a little bad about playing on Robyn's sensibilities, knowing she'd empathise with over-enthusiasm, but I needed to know what was going on in the zoo.

"I hear you! I was over the moon when I was given this job. Zookeepers don't often get to talk to the public all that much, but this job is the exact opposite. I chat until the cows come home!"

I silently pushed thoughts of this being my worst nightmare away.

"The expansion project is great. It's supposed to be really educational. The zoo has loads of great contacts with exotic pet owners and so on. By exotic, I don't mean things like big cats, but more like unusual pets and rare breeds. It's actually starting this week. We're going to have a Savannah cat owner come in. That's a domestic cat crossed with a serval. A lot of people get them because they look exotic, but they actually take a lot of hard work and commitment to care for." She beamed again. "That's why we want to educate people who are thinking about getting one!"

"That sounds really responsible." I was genuinely impressed and chided myself for being predisposed to believing that a larger zoo was an animal factory that didn't care for animals, only profit margins. There were always people within organisations who cared a great deal about their animals, and I knew I was in the presence of one such person. I felt a little stab of guilt over what could happen to her, should the zoo's reputation be damaged beyond repair, if all I'd heard about illegal smuggling was true. However, I was equally certain that if I'd been able to ask Robyn what she thought was the right thing to do, she'd make the same decision I had.

We worked cleaning out animal enclosures until lunchtime, and I was introduced to a mind-numbing amount of identical questions and misinformation repeated over and over by parents, as they consistently mistook animals' genders and even the different types of animal - in spite of the information notices. I didn't hate children, but I also had no desire to spend every day surrounded by hordes of screaming kids, who loved nothing more than to chase the goats and try to grab the rabbits. I spent most of my time asking children to not be so rough and explaining why animals needed to be treated with care. Every time I did so, Robyn would shoot me a big thumbs-up. Somehow, it made everything less annoying. I was grateful for my new partner.

By the time Robyn said I could take first lunch break, we'd already had five children leave the pet zone with half-eaten clothing, and ten cases of bitten fingers courtesy of the donkeys and the goats - who honestly gave as good as they got.

I said a cheery goodbye and made my way back to the staffroom.

The room was already pretty full up when I arrived. In spite of Robyn's assurances that I would soon get to know everyone, I definitely felt overwhelmed by the number of keepers Corbyn Manor employed. I thought it was going to be a tough enough challenge just to figure out who was doing a good job of looking after their animals, and who had room for improvement - let alone getting to the bottom of who, if any of them, were implicated in the smuggling operation. I took a deep breath and made myself think of where the best place to start might be. Big cats, reptiles, birds... they were all popular and had any number of possible fates. The illegal exotic pet trade and medicine market in China were just two of the terrible options. It was awful to even consider, but if I wanted to catch the people behind these terrible crimes, I would have to think the same way they did.

"Hey, new girl... what's your name?" a voice shouted out above the clamour of the staffroom.

Everyone fell silent and stared at me.

"I'm M... Molly," I said, stammering slightly as I came close to forgetting my false name. Talk about falling at the first hurdle!

Next came a whole flurry of names and occupations that I struggled to keep up with. The primate keepers were as nice as Robyn had implied. All of them had a sort of friendly scruffiness to them and relaxed mannerisms that let you know they were easy-going folk. Unfortunately, the same couldn't be said for all of the keepers. Rosa, the woman I'd spoken to briefly this morning, had an equally frosty looking colleague named Lee, but the third big cat keeper, Harry, looked a little friendlier and even managed a smile in my direction. The two amphibian keepers and reptile keeper were introduced, and while I still found myself weirded out by Kel and his reptile colleague, Herbert, Rowena (the quick acting alligator hero) bucked my experience of creepy crawly keepers, by looking completely normal.

The fowl keepers were a couple named Bill and Freya, aquatic animals were cared for by Gareth, hoofed animals were handled by Rai, and care of the other various mammals and outlying animals was split between Heather, Tesla, and Ricky.

Then there were all of the other zookeepers and apprentices who didn't have specialities. This group made up a large part of the staff and had names many and numerous that I struggled to memorise.

Finally, the man who'd shouted out the question introduced himself as Callum, Corbyn Manor's head-keeper. He extended a hand and I shook it, still dazed by the number of keepers this zoo employed. I was almost too distracted to notice the sparkle in his eye when he welcomed me to the zoo and commented on my obvious love for kids and fluffy animals. I realised he knew the truth.

For a second, I was miffed. This was supposed to be a secret operation to uncover areas that needed improvement, as far as animal care standards and zookeepers were concerned, at Corbyn Manor. But then I realised it was probably better to have the boss onside. As head-keeper, he was undoubtedly already trusted by management, but staff could be putting on a show while he was around. The standards of animal care would be harder to cover up, but I wasn't really here to criticise, just to give feedback. Everyone, even me, needed a second opinion every now and then.

After introductions were out of the way, I spent some time chatting to various keepers over lunch about their animals and everything about Corbyn Manor. Whilst I struggled to keep up with their names, I was immediately aware of how someone with the same level of job as I had was more likely to be open when head-keeper Callum was out of the way. I didn't learn anything too juicy, but there were definitely a few things that I was warned of that would be making my final report. I knew a lot could be done to make life better for the keepers themselves. A happy zoo was not just achieved on animal care alone! You had to care for your staff.

Auryn texted me halfway through my lunch break to tell me he had a break, too.

We met up in the picnic area of the zoo. I raised my eyebrows at the green and blue splatters that covered his already brightly coloured t-shirt. I received a scowl in return.

"So, it turns out I'm a glorified children's entertainer," he said. "They don't even take my scary zombie impression seriously."

"I'm not too far off that myself," I replied, thinking about how most of our time was spent stopping children from being too rough with the animals.

"It can't be as bad as what I'm doing. I'm supposed to be reviewing their events, but I'm stuck with a bunch of preschoolers who think throwing paint at each other is more fun than putting it on the paper. How is painting anything to do with Halloween?"

I inwardly raised an eyebrow at Auryn's lack of parental instinct. Much like me, he had endless adoration to lavish on animals, but when it came to kids, he liked them to remain a safe distance away. Perhaps that would change when Tiff's baby was born, but I, too, knew the dread that a pack of kids brought.

"What event are you running today?" I asked.

Auryn shrugged. "Cheap childcare apparently. The parents have a season pass to this place. They come in here and ditch the kids for the day at the weekends and in the holidays whilst they go off to do their own thing. They're not even in the zoo!"

"That's cheaper than childcare?"

Auryn nodded. "The alarming thing is, it actually is. It's not supposed to happen. We're not supposed to take kids off for the whole day. Children's activities are meant to engage the parents, too, but I can see why they don't want to stick around. Everything we do is completely irrelevant to the zoo. It's just throwing paint around and cutting and sticking paper and other mundane faux craft activities. There's nothing to do with the animals, it all happens in one boring kid's zone and no one learns anything. It's barely Halloween-themed! The rest of the staff look bored to heck. I'm bored, and I've only been doing it for a few hours!" He took a deep calming breath. "I just think it could be better. So much better."

"Then you've already done some good work," I told him with a smile.

His expression cleared from stressed out to calm. "I suppose you're right. If it were my zoo…" He trailed off with a happier look, already lost in ideas of how to improve things. "The real problem is, everyone here thinks I'm another average-Joe who's landed a job as a kid's entertainer for Halloween half-term. I feel so powerless."

I nodded. "I think I'm realising what makes our zoos so great," I said, being sure to keep my voice low, in case of listening ears. "A small size place where everyone gets to have a say means that our staff don't feel the way we do right now. It's a happier place."

"Definitely. But a bigger zoo shouldn't mean that things can't be good for everyone who works in it. Things can change."

"I hope they will," I replied. It was, after all, what we were here for. The zoo may think that they were commissioning us to report on staff productivity, animal care, and cuts and improvements to services offered, but I was fast seeing that a large part of our suggestions would be that conditions for the staff they employed were not up to scratch. With a bit of luck, management would listen and realise that, in order for the zoo to be improved, conditions for their staff needed to be fixed first.

I glanced down at the time on my phone and shot a regretful look in Auryn's direction. "Once more unto the breach…"

Auryn rolled his eyes. We both exchanged a pitying glance before going our separate ways.

Just what have we got ourselves into? I wondered… and not for the first time today.

My phone rang just as I finished shutting the donkeys in their stable for the night. Rain and colder temperatures were forecast as autumn began to turn towards winter, and donkeys' coats were not waterproof. Nasty conditions, such as rain scald and mud fever, could easily occur during the winter months if the once-desert-dwelling breed was left out in the elements without proper care.

"Connie, is everything okay?" I asked when I answered the phone after discovering it was my chef calling.

"No, not really…" she said and heaved in a breath that sounded thick with emotion.

"What's happened?" I asked, wondering if there'd been some terrible disaster in the restaurant. Connie had always struck me as an unflappable and highly capable woman. It must have been something awful to shake her.

"They think I did it. They think that I killed that poor man," she said, finally spitting it out.

"You mean Joe Harvey?" I was sorry to even have to check, but I wanted to make sure that no one else had died.

"Yes! The papers are publishing all kinds of things about me. I don't know how they know, but they think I killed him because of my past. I have no idea how they could have found out. I never wanted to hide it, but it's not the kind of thing that gets you employed." She sighed, and I heard her misery down the phone line.

I was struggling to make sense of what she was saying. "What have the press found out about your past?" That seemed like a good place to start.

"You haven't seen? Oh." She took another steadying breath. "I am so sorry for not telling you, but I try not to think of it these days. I've put it behind me, but clearly I was wrong to think that it was all forgotten. The truth is…" I braced myself for some terrible truth about my chef that would shake me to the core. "…I'm a murderer," she finished.

I did some rapid blinking. Had Connie just confessed on the phone to me? I was so confused! "Who did you murder?" I asked, wanting to get this straight.

"It was my ex-husband, about ten years ago now. He was very abusive. I didn't see it at the time. Looking back now..." She sighed again. "One day, he got into a rage. I was certain he was going to kill me. I managed to grab a knife from the unit, and when he ran at me, I was holding it, and he sort of ran onto it. It sounds like the most unbelievable story in the world. I know that. I've been told it enough times by the prosecution in court, but it is what happened. Fortunately, the jury agreed that it was self-defence. My injuries were pretty impossible to overlook. After it all happened, I rebuilt my life and did my best to forget all about it. I'm sorry if you think I pulled the wool over your eyes to get the job."

"Don't think that for a minute!" I said, jumping to the defence of my star chef. "I know you did what you believed was right... you did what you had to. It's the press who are in the wrong for dredging up my employees' pasts in order to dig up something juicy." I bit my lip. "It's my fault for being famous. I'm so sorry..."

"I'm the one who's sorry!" Connie batted back.

We exchanged a few more claims for the blame before we started to laugh.

"Look - I know it sounds cliché, but this will all blow over in no time at all. If you are willing to weather the storm, then I think there'll be brighter days ahead. You will always have a job at The Wild Spot. It wouldn't work without you!" I assured her.

"But what about all of this bad press? Half the public probably think I'm a mad axe murderer! It could ruin your restaurant."

I thought about it and found that I was smiling. "Well... Halloween is on the way."

"How does that help?" Connie sounded genuinely exasperated.

"I mean there's no need to worry. No one will be put off coming to the restaurant. If anything, I bet people will flock there. Sometimes bad publicity is your best publicity. People are nasty, curious beasts… I reckon bookings will double."

Over the next few weeks, it actually transpired that bookings quadrupled. Whilst I worried a lot about Connie's mental health, being permanently reminded of a past she'd wanted to forget, she continued to assure me she was fine… and the restaurant continued to boom.

After my conversation with Connie Breeze, my mind continued to be plagued with thoughts about secret pasts. I would never in a million years have dreamed that capable and efficient Connie had been pushed to kill someone, but once the circumstances had been explained, I could understand it. All kinds of unexpected people did all kinds of unexpected things when they were put into certain situations. It was only when you found yourself in that moment that you discovered how you were going to act. If Connie hadn't defended herself, she could have been the one who'd been killed.

When I'd arrived home, my thoughts had moved onto Detective Gregory and his past. Was he another man plagued by circumstances that now made him appear to be something he wasn't? I had to find out the truth. My best friend was married to a man who definitely had secrets - no matter how he'd come to have them. And if he'd concealed that past for any reason, beyond it being in her best interests, he would have hell to pay.

"The truth… it has to be the truth," I muttered, knowing

that anything less would put me on the same level as the press in Connie's case. I didn't want to tear up a relationship because of idle gossip and ill-researched suspicions. I needed cold hard facts.

I started by writing down all that I thought I knew about Alex Gregory.

He previously worked somewhere in Brighton as part of the police force.

He owns a gun that he has easy access to.

He has enemies.

Joe Harvey claimed Detective Gregory worked as a mercenary - although he hadn't known if he was currently employed by anyone.

The man who'd broken into his house had claimed that Alex Gregory had got his position on the police force by nefarious means.

I bit the top of the pen, looking down at my list. Unfortunately, I could immediately see that there were only three things that could be called facts, or were at least likely to be facts. The rest was just conjecture and rumour.

With a glance at the hour (which was late) I shook off my sleepiness and got to work. If Alex Gregory had buried any skeletons, I was going to dig them up.

I did some more pen chewing before I got stuck in. It wasn't the first time that it had occurred to me that Alex might have noticed Joe at his wedding the same way Joe had noticed him. Joe had never exactly been forthcoming with the truth, and perhaps he'd known something more about Alex Gregory than he'd shared with me on that day. Something deadly.

I didn't want to have to contemplate it, but I did. I wondered if my best friend's husband was currently investigating a murder that he'd committed himself.

5

SECRETS, SPIES, AND ALIBIS

"**H**owdy, partner! Have you seen all of the new recruits?" Robyn greeted me when I rolled into the pet zone with bags beneath my eyes.

My research session had continued well into the early hours of the morning but had yielded few results. All I'd been able to find using the internet was that Alex Gregory had worked for the Brighton police force in a position that was surprisingly junior to the one he now held. Whilst it corre- lated with Jim Smith's claims that Alex had been promoted beyond the norm, in itself, it wasn't particularly damning. My usual next step would be to go to Katya and ask her to look into it further, but I didn't think I had that option anymore.

"New recruits?" I queried, realising that Robyn had sort of asked me a question.

"Yeah! I thought your job was the only one going, and even that was a surprise. I've been angling for help for a year! Today I came into work to find out that a whole load of people have been hired under some new 'visitor experience' directive. I think that means they're going to be checking up on all of us. I doubt they'll be very welcome." She shook her head. "I know they're only here to spy, but I feel sorry for the poor guys. No one will want to share a doughnut with them, that's for sure."

I was doing my best to squash down my feelings of panic, alarm, and outrage whilst she told me all of this. Just what did Corbyn Manor think it was playing at?! They'd employed us pretty grudgingly, if truth be told, and now they'd suddenly decided to hire a whole team of people to very obviously spy on their staff? It made no sense at all.

"I'm sure we'll be fine. No one's going to cut the pet zone. For starters, no one ever wants to work here - apart from us two fuzzy lovers - and secondly, it's popular as heck! Kids and adults love being able to actually touch animals. You can't do that if you've only got tigers and bears and what have you."

I managed a weak smile in response to her assurances that we wouldn't lose our jobs. After Robyn's little speech I was feeling even more anxious about what she'd say if she found out that I was just as guilty as this new department the zoo had inexplicably hired.

"There's one of them now! They even look like bad news, don't they?" Robyn said, the cheer going out of her voice for a moment.

I followed her gaze to the man walking past the entrance of the pet zone. He was dressed in a suit that seemed out of place at a zoo, and there was a distinct absence of humour on his face.

I knew exactly who he was.

Mr Flannigan looked over and saw us watching him. When he saw me, he dragged the corners of his mouth up into a smile. It was horrible to look at.

"Molly, isn't it? I hear you're new here. Would you mind talking to me about your first impressions of the zoo?"

Robyn made a tiny coughing sound that I could only assume expressed her disgust in the most Robyn-like way (which was to say - utterly inoffensively).

I grudgingly nodded and walked with the MI5 agent away from the pet zone.

"I like your disguise," Flannigan said in his usual snarky way.

"It was necessary."

"I wouldn't have known it was you. Fortunately, I had prior knowledge, courtesy of Tiffany Gregory," he said, listing my best friend's new name. There was a slight smirk on his lips when he said it, and I wondered if it had anything to do with his knowledge about her husband... or was I being paranoid? "In the light of what has happened to your employee, and what we've since uncovered, surveillance is needed... for your protection," he added, unconvincingly.

"Because of the death threat?"

"Yes... of course. Because of that, and something else."

I waited.

"We should discuss it somewhere else... it's something you should see."

After that mysterious pronouncement he marched off. I presumed I was supposed to follow him. I turned and shrugged back in Robyn's direction, knowing I probably didn't look too happy about it. At least that would go in my favour. However, I wasn't convinced how long my cover would last. I'd worried that Auryn's and my simultaneous arrival would be enough to set suspicious tongues wagging, but when you added in a whole raft of new employees, I worried that our own positions were all too transparent. We'd hoped to gain trust and confidences in order to uncover the truth about the dark hidden side that we suspected existed at Corbyn Manor. Now we could find ourselves permanent outcasts.

I didn't miss the irony of the situation. Hadn't I been a thorn in MI5's side during their past operations when I'd stuck my nose in where they thought it shouldn't belong? Now it was their turn to scupper my own investigation.

We walked into the staff-only area of the zoo, winding through seemingly endless walkways that connected the many animal enclosures. It wasn't long before Flannigan turned down towards a cluster of what appeared to be disused storage shacks. He walked up to the largest one and opened the door.

Four faces turned to look at us when we entered. I was none too happy to realise I recognised three of them. Two of the men had worked on the faux security team at the zoo they'd set up with the main purpose of spying on me and my then-publishing company. The third man was my ex-boyfriend, Lowell. I'd already had the displeasure of seeing him turn up on my doorstep, but it was still a cold punch to the stomach to realise he'd actually be working in close proximity to me.

The only presence I missed was Katya's. As soon as I'd seen Flannigan, and had realised just who this mysterious new department really was, I'd hoped that she would be on the case, as she had been part of the very select few who'd known the ins and outs of the publishing sting operation. However, I had known that we'd not left each other on the best of terms. It seemed likely that she'd asked permission to not be involved with this side of the operation... or maybe she was working on another case. I was completely out of the loop now I'd lost my friend and only trusted contact.

"You brought her in here?" That was my delightful ex-boyfriend talking. He looked at me like I was a particularly dangerous criminal who might attack him at any second. I glared back.

"She should see the video. We're not getting anywhere with it, and it was intended for her. She'll know what it means," Flannigan said with a dismissive shrug.

I looked back and forth between the two men, finding no fondness for either of them.

"What video?" I hated being talked above.

Lowell turned back to the computer screen he'd been facing when we'd entered the room. "That package I intercepted was a DVD recorded by the late Rich Summers - the man you knew as Jordan Barnes and then Joe Harvey." He shot me a look when he mentioned those names in tandem.

I kept my face blank. I'd already told them that I'd had no idea those men were one and the same and I wasn't going to crack now. I couldn't see any way that sharing the truth would do anything other than get me into serious trouble.

I hadn't counted on Joe himself letting the cat out of the bag.

"Right. Well, here's the video. I'm sure we'll all be fascinated to hear your thoughts after you've watched it..." Lowell pressed play and Joe Harvey's image jumped onto the screen. To my bemusement, I recognised his surroundings. Somehow, without my noticing, he'd filmed it at The Lucky Zoo in front of the living wall that climbed up the side of the barn conversion.

"If you're watching this... I'm dead," he began, taking his sunglasses off when he made that shocking announcement. Joe was dressed in a white suit and I wondered if this was all a reference to a film.

Once he'd allowed enough time for the viewer to get over the shock announcement, he continued on a more personal note. "I've made quite a number of these videos over the years. As with the others, I hope that no one will ever see this, but it's always better to be prepared. In the event of my death, this video will have been sent to you, Madi." His eyes focused on the screen and I noticed that he wasn't wearing the blue contact lenses he'd worn all the time he was acting as Joe Harvey. Instead, hazel and gold was back in evidence, and I found myself remembering the man I'd first met in the coffee shop in Cornwall.

"If you are watching this video, then I'm pleased to say it was one made in a happy time. There aren't too many loose ends to tie up." He flashed the camera a devilish grin. *Easy for you to say!* I silently thought, peeved by the amount of trouble Joe's death had got me into.

"The last time we properly spoke, we were working on a plan to defy your great oppressors." He shook his head. "I've had my fair share of adversaries, but this time it's tough. I think I might be in some serious trouble." He grinned again, showing his sense of humour. "For one group to have a monopoly is serious, and I'm going to help you put an end to it." Unfortunately, whilst I knew he was mocking my small-town enemies, this video had been watched and scrutinised by MI5. They probably assumed he was referring to something far more serious than other PR companies and members of the Lords of the Downs - the exclusive gentlemen-only club, of which Auryn was a member.

"Anyway, here's my advice for how to deal with it. The best thing to put a stop to overarching influencers is for a rival to enter the fray. Competition is healthy. You'll soon shake them off their perches. As for my enemies, if my death was not natural, I'm afraid I can't help you much. I've rubbed a lot of people up the wrong way - more so recently than ever before. Both sides could be plotting my downfall at this very moment. You know that, Madi." His gaze softened for a moment. I silently cursed him as I realised that his last remark was not cryptic at all and would certainly be taken as evidence by MI5 that I knew a heck of a lot more than I'd let on.

"However, I can offer a word of advice. Never trust someone who turns their back on those they're supposed to be loyal to, even if they renounce them. If they've turned their coat once, who's to say they won't do it twice? Myself excepted, of course." He winked and walked sideways along the living wall, reaching out speculatively to touch one of the leafy green plants with striking red stems. He swept a strand of his hair back from his ear and turned back to the camera. "I'm relying on you if my death is shrouded in mystery. You've done it before, and you can do it again. Find the truth - no matter who tries to stop you. And don't believe all of the bad press, either. Find out for yourself." There was a warmth in his eyes that I knew all too well. Joe was showing his feelings for me one last time - feelings that I'd never truly understood.

His expression darkened and something ugly crossed his face. "And if this video has fallen into someone else's hands... let me tell you exactly how you'll live to regre-"

The screen went blank. I looked at Lowell and he looked back at me. There was no apology on his face for cutting off the video early, but I could hazard a good guess as to what Joe had been going on to say, and it certainly wasn't polite.

"Unless I'm much mistaken, you know rather more than you've been telling us?" Flannigan said with ill-concealed glee.

I shifted uncomfortably in the presence of these four men, who definitely had the power to lock me up for a very long time. The problem was, they believed I was protecting Joe. In truth, I was protecting my own investigation into the animal smuggling. The reason? I didn't trust British Intelligence as far as I could throw them. Even Joe's video had hinted that a double agent could be where the blame rested for his untimely death. Hadn't it been widely acknowledged that someone had betrayed MI5's plans to Rock and Roll Publishing prior to the sting that was supposed to seize the money launderers? I hadn't seen or heard any signs of repercussions, so I could only assume that the blame had been put elsewhere. That or (more likely, I thought) the double agent was still at large and was very skilled at covering their tracks.

I bit my lip, knowing I couldn't say anything in the present company. Two of the men in the room had known about that sting before it had happened. Either one of them could be the traitor. *What about Alex Gregory?* a little voice in my head piped up. He hadn't been involved in that operation, to my knowledge, but was it simply coincidence that had seen him installed as Gigglesfield's detective so soon after the bust had collapsed? I wasn't saying that he was the traitor, but he could certainly have had some prior reason to want Joe Harvey dead. Perhaps he'd been the first to figure out who my PR and marketing man really was.

The problem was, I wasn't feeling overly trusting of anyone right now.

I silently wished for the umpteenth time that Katya hadn't estranged herself from me. Now would have been the perfect moment to compare notes again about the man calling himself Alex Gregory. She hadn't known his name, but what about his face?

"Well, Ms Amos?" Mr Flannigan prompted, using the incorrect name and title just to irk me, I was sure.

I remembered he'd asked an exceedingly awkward question. "I was made aware of Joe Harvey's previous identity," I said, being careful with my words. "He came to me looking for work claiming that he wanted a fresh start and a way out of his criminal lifestyle. He managed to persuade me to give him a chance… and that's what I did."

"You gave an internationally wanted criminal a chance,"

Lowell said, disbelief massively evident in his voice. In his tone I heard a great deal of hurt that I would give Joe an opportunity to redeem himself when I hadn't afforded Lowell the same chance. My little mistruth made me itch inside. I hated the double standards I was presenting to them, but I couldn't tell them the whole truth - not when I strongly suspected that all of this somehow tied together... and it had resulted in one man's death.

"What did you make of the video?" Flannigan asked, still keeping that amused 'I'm better than you' expression on his face.

I made a show of thinking about it. "I believe he really had changed his ways. I have a problem with a local group of powerful men, who have a great deal of influence over local businesses. I went to Joe for help, and even in death, he's given me an excellent suggestion. I think I'm going to act upon it." Even as the words left my mouth I realised I meant it. I'd been pondering the Lords of the Downs problem for some time, but Joe's idea just might work. A rival club could push the men off their pedestal.

"That's all you have to say?" Flannigan feigned sadness. Behind him, Lowell turned away with a single head-shake that indicated his view.

"That's all I have to say," I confirmed and walked out of the shed.

The next few days were spent keeping a low profile. With MI5 on the prowl and generally making a nuisance of themselves, I wanted the days to pass as smoothly as possible. I shut out all of the watching eyes from the new department, who to the uninformed viewer must have seemed inordinately interested in the pet zone, and I got on with looking after the animals I was in charge of. It was actually nice to be a zookeeper and nothing else (as far as my colleagues knew). I liked Robyn and, together, we came up with some great ideas of how to make the pet zone even better in the future. She warned me straightaway that we'd have a hard time lobbying management for that kind of thing, but I had a slight advantage there, didn't I?

Auryn and I also did our best to integrate. I was friendly and helpful to everyone I met, and Auryn offered to cover lunch breaks and take on the most troublesome children that they had dumped on them. We did our best to stay in everyone's good books, and all the while, we searched for the wolves amongst the sheep.

It was Liberty the lynx who inspired me to turn my attention to the big cat keepers. Unfortunately, prior to his death, Joe had kept his cards close to his chest when it came to revealing the kinds of animals that were generally smuggled out of the country. Or perhaps he'd even assumed that it was so blatantly obvious, he hadn't bothered to tell us.

All I knew was that the evidence suggested big cats were definitely on the cards for the smugglers. Unfortunately, the big cat keepers at Corbyn Manor were as unapproachable as it got. They hung out in their clique and eyed anyone who approached them with disdain. When I'd expressed an interest in getting to know them, Robyn had laughed in this strangled way that hinted at major animosity. I knew by now that it would take a heck of a lot to make her feel that way about anyone. They must have been particularly nasty to her, and every instinct warned me to steer clear of this bad bunch.

It was too bad that I also had them pegged as the lot most likely to be heinous criminals.

In the end, I resorted to hanging around the big cat enclosures, hoping to bump into the keepers. Mostly, I received the brush off, but I did glean one or two pieces of useful information. The first was that the keepers, for all their snobbery, were not actually brilliant at their jobs. I'd never been a big cat keeper, but I'd certainly gained enough experience of good ones to know poor examples when I saw them.

On the face of it, the enclosures were clean, and the animals didn't look unwell, but as soon as you looked a little closer, you realised that you'd summed up all the work they were doing in those two observations. The cats were splendidly isolated on their large squares of grass with a few shrubs dotted around and a couple of perfunctory platforms. There was no engagement, no interest, and nothing to remind them that they were big cats. Even though I knew my real purpose for being at the zoo was to uncover a darker truth, what I'd seen was very definitely going to be included in my report.

The other thing I'd learned was that Kusha, one of the resident female tigers, was pregnant and expected to give birth any time in the next couple of weeks. I'd already witnessed firsthand at Avery Zoo how unscrupulous keepers were able to fudge the numbers when it came to new arrivals. I knew that if I wanted to make sure every single tiger cub was accounted for, I would have to find a way to be present for the birth.

After many failed attempts to bond with Lee and Rosa, and a few chats with the slightly friendlier Harry, I knew it wasn't going to be easy.

The worst part about working at Corbyn Manor was having to see Lowell every day. After finally learning the truth about everything, I'd thought I'd told him goodbye for the last time, but here he was, right under my nose. It was like being back at Avery Zoo when he'd been pretending to work as a builder. I'd figured out pretty quickly that he was something else entirely (although I'd been wrong about his real profession). Yet again, I was forced to conceal the truth about a man I retained significant doubts about.

Auryn didn't like it either. He seemed to think that Lowell still had unresolved feelings for me and that his assignment to this job was no accident. He'd even gone so far as to suggest that Lowell himself had been responsible for the death threat I'd received - slipping it in amongst the mail when he'd handed the pile over to me after extracting Joe's parcel. While it would explain the presence of only Lowell's and my fingerprints on the envelope, I found it hard to entertain the idea that Lowell wanted to have anything to do with me. All I'd seen was resentment.

It had, however, made me wonder if Auryn was on the right track... but for the wrong reasons. Lowell had been involved in the sting operation. He'd repeatedly lied to me - although, he still claimed it was only what he'd been told to do. All the same, I wasn't ruling out the possibility that Lowell was a traitor, not only to me, but to the people he worked with.

Could I contemplate him being a murderer, too? Of that, I was less sure. Lowell had betrayed me in the worst possible way, but I still believed that some of what we'd shared had at least been partly genuine. I wanted to believe that he wasn't a killer.

Today, I was doing my best to document all of the rabbits currently in residence in their vast green, hilly enclosure. There were still some rabbits that were barely more than kittens and they had to be accounted for, correctly aged, and scheduled for neutering, or the rabbit corner would be inundated with yet more new arrivals. The difficulty was, a lot of them looked a lot more like their wild cousins than their domestic counterparts, which led to some confusion. For one, they all looked the same - brown and with big eyes. Secondly, I couldn't be certain (beyond their decided lack of affection for humans) that they'd already been fixed. A lack of affection for humans didn't even mean they were definitely wild. I wouldn't have blamed any rabbit living in these parts for displaying a healthy suspicion of humans, given what they put up with on a daily basis.

I was mulling over the conundrum of whether or not to round up all of the wild-looking rabbits and have a vet look them over (and potentially return any genuine wayward wild rabbits to where they belonged) or to just hope for the best and see if any new litters were born, or not, when someone cleared their throat behind me. I turned around to discover Lowell standing by the edge of the enclosure with a clipboard in his hand. The rabbit enclosure was closed for the hour. Robyn and I were supposed to be counting up bunnies (and then comparing notes). She'd popped off for a break, so we were strangely alone in the cordoned off enclosure. And I was painfully aware of it.

"What can I do for you?" I asked, figuring that politeness cost nothing - no matter how fed up you were with the person you were talking to.

"You can tell me the truth. You owe me that much at least." He levelled his dark gaze at me, and just for a moment, I looked back into his eyes and remembered our happier times.

"Do I?" I said, swapping politeness for pettiness. At least I'd tried, right?

"Were you planning to enter a life of crime with your old literary agent, just to spite me?"

I made a sound of disgust. "I don't do anything for you. I thought you were out of my life forever."

Lowell nodded like he'd believed it too. "Some things

never change, as much as you might want them to," he said, rather philosophically. I promised myself I wouldn't think on it later. Everything Lowell said meant nothing to me.

"Do I look like I'm entering a life of crime?" I gestured around at the rabbits, who were innocuously watching our progressively more heated exchange.

"You tell me," Lowell said with a glitter in his eyes that told me I'd just fallen for whatever trap he'd been carefully laying. "Why would a successful comic book author and zoo owner suddenly accept a job as a lowly zookeeper at a new zoo... and wear a disguise to do it?"

I shot him a withering look. If that was the best he could come up with... "I'm sure you've already spoken to management about my real role here. I like to help people and animals. Working as a consultant was all I ever really wanted to do. Everything else has been the icing on the cake, but I've missed this kind of work. I'm guessing it was when you found out about my job that you decided to steal the idea for your own?"

Lowell shrugged. "It seemed like a plausible thing for a zoo to commission - seeing as they'd already done exactly that in secret. We just flashed our IDs and demanded they set up a department and employ us all. Then we made them sign The Act."

I nearly rolled my eyes. 'The Act' was the Secret Service's cover all eventualities weapon. Silence could be bought by forcing people to sign a bit of paper.

"Now you know the extent of my criminal career, if you call a little bit of espionage criminal." I pulled a face. "I know it's hardly honest... but if the keepers are hardworking and good keepers, there's nothing for them to worry about." I couldn't help but glance in the direction of where I could hear Robyn's laughter as she chatted to someone on her way back. When all was said and done, I'd be very sorry if she thought I'd betrayed her.

My ex-boyfriend nodded. "That's all there is to it then. It's nothing to do with this zoo being a hotbed of animal smugglers."

6

DEAD ENDS

I froze."What do you mean?" I knew I'd fallen for something, but that didn't mean I couldn't climb back out.

For a moment Lowell and I remained in deadlock, each watching the other for signs of weakness.

In the end, Lowell's gaze softened. "Katya told me why you're really here at the zoo. She said you're trying to find evidence for a supposed smuggling ring who are operating in the UK and using the zoos to source their animals."

The shock and outrage must have shown on my face because Lowell quickly continued. "Don't blame Katya. She was doing us both a favour. I knew you got on well together so I asked her to keep an eye out for you all this time." He raised his hands in presumptive defence. "Not to spy on you! Just to make sure you were okay and not getting into too much trouble." His dark eyebrows lifted a little when he said that and I realised he must have heard that, in spite of Katya's best efforts, I'd got into plenty.

"She told me about the animal smugglers because she thought I could help. I think at first she didn't want to believe what you were telling her - especially because you wouldn't say who your source was. She knows your history and thought someone was pulling your leg." He shrugged apologetically. "But, she looked into what you have and found a few things that seemed to suggest there may be some truth to it. She came to me because she knows I've got a fair amount of experience with smugglers and breaking into their operations."

I remembered back to Lowell telling me he'd worked on a cross-channel gun smuggling operation. That had been what had seen him recruited for MI5.

"I suppose your superiors know about it, too." I was well-used to Lowell's by the book attitude. It had been the same attitude that had kept him from telling me the truth about our relationship, even after I'd guessed most of it.

He shook his head. "I've kept it to myself. The way I see it, there's not enough hard evidence to take it any further. I don't see any reason why we can't find the evidence for it and then hand it over to the authorities." He looked appealingly at me.

I found myself nodding. Hadn't that been what I'd hoped for all along? I'd been unable to turn the case over to the authorities because there was nothing more than rumour and a wayward lynx to back up my claims. Once I'd found and gathered proof that all of this was happening, I'd fully intended to pass it along... hadn't I? I silently admitted to myself that I hadn't thought that far ahead. But now that I did, it made the most sense. I wasn't hunting for glory. I wanted justice for the animals. Lowell's suggestion was logical.

But that didn't mean I had to like it.

"I don't trust you," I told him, speaking plainly.

Lowell nodded. "I know. But you do need me." There was something smug in his voice that pushed me over the edge. It was something that made me think he wasn't just talking about animal smugglers.

"I can handle it fine," I told him, turning away in what I hoped was a dismissive move.

"I'm sorry," Lowell said a second later.

I turned back, surprised to hear the words exit his mouth.

"I made a huge mistake. I know that now. It was a mistake that cost me having you in my life. Even though I was pushed towards you, I wasn't lying when I told you how I felt. I can see why you wouldn't believe me, but it's true." His dark eyes were full of regret that I realised he'd been hiding beneath the stone and ice he'd directed at me since we'd been pushed together again. "But I'm glad you're happy."

"Thank you," I said, realising it was the time to be decent. Lowell had just opened his heart to me. It didn't change anything now, and deep down I was certain that somehow, Auryn and I would have ended up together anyway. We were meant to be.

Lowell looked down at the ground, where a bunch of rabbits had gathered and were looking up curiously at him. He reached a hand down towards them and they whiffled their noses his way before allowing him to stroke their ears. I silently reflected that any person who animals tended to trust couldn't be too terrible - although, the rabbits were well used to putting up with all kinds of tiny psychopaths.

I couldn't shake that deep-rooted feeling of mistrust. I could think of plenty of reasons why Lowell had the potential to be the double-agent and his knowledge and experience of smuggling didn't go in his favour when I thought about it that way. He'd supposedly worked to catch the gun smugglers, but what if he'd been turned all that time ago and had been working for the money launderers ever since? Lowell had been headhunted for intelligence during that case, but what if they were the second lot who'd headhunted him?

I bit my lip, wondering if I was right, or if I was simply paranoid when it came to all matters relating to Lowell. Joe's voice seemed to fill my head for a moment, repeating what he'd said on the video. *Never trust someone who turns their back on those they're supposed to be loyal to, even if they renounce them. If they've turned their cloak once, who's to say they won't do it twice?* As far as I was concerned, that statement definitely applied to Lowell. I knew the world wasn't as black and white as people liked to make out. Even a sense of morals did not rule Lowell out from being the double-agent and believing that he was the one in the right, but it did make him even harder to trust.

"What do you know about Detective Alex Gregory of the Gigglesfield police force?" I asked, seeing a chance to test Lowell's supposed loyalty and to answer a question that had been bugging me for a long time.

"I don't know any one by that name," he replied with an easy shrug.

"But you do know him," I guessed. I'd been with Lowell long enough to know when he was evading the truth. He'd done it to me enough times.

Lowell shrugged again. "Does anyone really know anyone, or even themselves?" I shot him a warning look. Now wasn't the time for vague philosophical statements. "I couldn't say. Why are you asking?"

"He just married my best friend," I said, watching Lowell's face carefully for any signs of surprise, horror, or amusement.

He kept it studiously blank. "I hope they have a happy marriage."

"So do I. But if I find out you knew anything…" I left the threat hanging. To be fair, it wasn't much of a threat. I'd lost all trust in Lowell a long time ago and there was nothing left to be removed from our relationship. Anyway, what could five foot nothing me do against someone the size of Lowell? The only thing I could think of was not agreeing to work with him on the animal smuggling case, but then... I hadn't agreed to work with him anyway, had I?

"We'll talk soon," Lowell announced and on that ominous note, he walked away and left me with the rabbits.

"What did the spy want?" Robyn asked frowning at Lowell's receding figure.

Her statement nearly made me jump out of my skin, before I remembered that Lowell was known to be spying on the zoo's staff. "He said he was thinking about getting a pet rabbit and wanted some advice."

Robyn shook her head. "These sneaks will try anything. I bet he wanted to catch you out."

"I'm certain that was it," I agreed, wholeheartedly.

Coming back to our house in the evenings was an interesting affair. The press were maintaining their fascination with the suspiciously well-publicised murder of Joe Barnes, and my potential involvement in it. Even though I hadn't been dragged in for questioning since the preliminary round, and wasn't being considered a suspect either (to my knowledge), the media were determined to dig up something - anything - that might hint otherwise. My fall from grace was a dramatic one, and one that I strongly suspected had been engineered.

They giveth and they taketh away, I thought to myself endlessly, remembering that my initial rise to fame had, to some extent at least, been implemented by MI5. Now, for their own ends, they'd decided to leak details that hinted I was the bad guy. I was saddened by the prospect of my short-lived comic career potentially coming to an end, but I was far more concerned that I was being set up for a very real fall... one that might result in my death. It seemed only too obvious to me that MI5 wanted Joe's old cronies to think I knew more than I was letting on... and then they would come for me. The Secret Service might believe it was the perfect trap, but I knew from experience with animals that bait often got mangled.

Auryn and I had taken to drawing our curtains at the front of the house and living round the back. Since the first press person had scaled the wall and met Rameses no one else had attempted it. Fortunately, the media's talent for exaggeration clearly extended to the report the photographer had passed on to his fellows. Otherwise, they'd have all realised Rameses was a teddy bear, not a tyrant.

"I'm off to the club meeting. I hope this doesn't go against my standing - all the bad press and whatnot," Auryn said in a false posh voice whilst rolling his eyes. At home we mocked the Lords of the Downs, but deep down we both knew that Auryn felt compelled to play ball, or everyone would suffer the consequences.

"Try to smarten up a bit. They might get some good photos we could put in the family album," I joked.

Auryn stuck his tongue out, wished me goodbye, and left the house.

I waited for the shouts of the media asking Auryn if he'd been my accomplice to murder to die down before I made my move.

With grim determination, I picked up my mobile phone and dialled the first person on my long list.

"Hi Georgina, how are you?" I asked when the high-flying lawyer picked up.

"Madi! So good to hear from you. I'm fantastic, thank you. Did you hear about all of the kerfuffle with dear departed Harry's will?" The amount of sarcasm she used here bordered on indecent, given that she was talking about a murdered man. There was no love lost between the ex-husband and wife.

"I know that he apparently gave it all to a British wildlife charity? That was incredibly generous of him…"

I could almost hear Georgina smile. "Quite a surprise, wasn't it? He should have learned to read things through before signing them. But that was ancient history. I never actually expected that will would be the one that was used when the time came…" She cleared her throat. "It was just another jab at getting even. We used to do it all the time when we were together."

"Has Felicity officially decided to contest it?" I asked, unsurprised if that were the case. Felicity Farley had been Harry Farley's wife up until his unfortunate death. She'd definitely been banking on inheriting a big chunk, if not all, of his family money.

Georgina chuckled. "Felicity and all the rest of them. Harry's family have come out of the woodwork like you wouldn't believe. Apparently, the family fortune is always passed on to other family members. That's how they stay rich and can afford to keep toying with little business ideas that never go anywhere." I silently raised my eyebrows at Georgina's reference to Farley and Sons estate agents. "They say there's no way it can all go to something as despicable as a charity - let alone the horror of something that actually preserves wildlife."

"Did they really say that?"

"They might as well have done," Georgina confirmed. "Of course, as soon as they found out that I was the one who put his will together, all hell broke loose. They're taking me to court over some jumped up charge they've looked up in a 'My First Law Degree' book. I almost pity them. They're going to spend more money on fancy lawyers than they'll ever get out of that will." I found myself admiring Georgina's infallible confidence in her own abilities.

"Will his money really go to the charity?"

"Oh, I should think so. I know my own work and there are no loopholes or get-outs. As I said, I assumed he'd make a fresh will years in the future when he had kids, or swapped wives again. To be honest, I thought he'd have had a new one made when he married Felicity. I don't think it was done in slight against her, I think Harry thought he was going to live forever. The only reason he had a will in the first place was because his father told him to stop being an irresponsible dolt and get one done. He palmed it off on me. I was angry enough at the time to make the changes I made, and then the fool skim read it and signed on the dotted line in front of a witness. There's no way they'll get out of it." For a second, she sounded apologetic, perhaps thinking that not all of Harry Farley's family was necessarily as bad as he'd been. "It'll be enough to pay the charity's CEOs a nice Christmas bonus, that's for sure," she finished in a dry tone.

There was a pause as she collected her thoughts and probably realised that I must have called her for some reason beyond a gossip. "What can I do for you? Need someone to get you off murder?"

"Not at the moment, thank you," I said, less amused than I might have been, due to the camping press outside of the house. "I'm actually calling to ask if you might want to be a part of a new club I'm setting up. It's more of a society really," I said, blustering a bit due to the lack of details I'd worked out.

"You're not trying to convert me to some crazy religion are you?" Georgina asked, sounding amused.

"No! I'm trying to set up a women-only club to compete with the Lords of the Downs. I don't think it's fair that a bunch of rich and successful men get to decide the fate of businesses run by ordinary men and women - who don't get to have a say."

"You should have led with that," Georgina informed me. "I'm in."

"Great!" I was just thrilled to have my first 'yes'. I'd spent many hours deliberating whether or not Joe's dying suggestion was a stupid one, or a brilliant one, and just how I was going to do it, before I'd figured that calling around was the most straightforward way. "Any ideas on a name?" I asked, deciding to push my luck a little bit.

"Quite a few, actually, but none that would be considered civil towards the men." There was a pause. "Ladies of the Common? You know... because we're common and not good enough for them."

I thought about it. "It sounds perfect." It was obviously setting us up as a competitor with a tongue-in-cheek feel that would let 'the lords' know exactly what we were intending to do.

"How many people have you got so far?" Georgina asked.

"You're the first person I've called."

"I'm flattered! You picked well. The only other person I could think of who might have a lower opinion of the Lords of the Downs would be Nigel Wickington's wife, Annemarie. Do you mind if I make a few calls of my own?"

I assured her that she would be welcome to send out invites. We definitely weren't going to be as exclusive in terms of membership as our male competitors were... and I thought it might just be where we derived our strength. "Annemarie was actually second on my list. They've got a meeting going on right now, so I wasn't sure if it was a good idea to call up while all of that was going on."

Georgina laughed. "I'd say it would be the best time. Annemarie is fed up with having to run around and fetch that boorish group of men tea and biscuits, like some glorified tea lady. She's a very successful businesswoman in her own right, you know! But you wouldn't know it the way those men treat her... I'll give her a call," she announced. "You should try..." She reeled off a list of names and numbers and I scrabbled to write them all down. According to Georgina, they'd all be terribly impressed to be receiving a call from *the* Madigan Amos (suspected murderer or not) and there was no way they'd say no to pretty much anything I asked of them.

Three names and numbers into Georgina's list and three strong yeses later, I realised that I had a club on my hands. We were really going to do it! The first thing everyone had said when I'd called and mentioned the idea and potential for rivalry was 'It's about time someone did something about them!" or words to that effect. I'd long suspected it, but now it was clear that I wasn't the only one who resented the power that a group of wealthy and powerful men had over the way things were run in our town and its surrounding satellites.

It was time to end their reign.

"You won't believe what happened whilst you were on lunch!" Robyn said, steaming up to me with a big smile on her face. I got the sense that she was about to tell me some bad news, but it was always tough to tell due to her bouncy personality.

"Did one of the goats finally manage to sever a finger and took the next step towards cannibalism?" It was surely only a matter of time...

Robyn shook her head. "Not yet, but it's nearly as bad as that! Jemima's been sitting on her eggs for a whole week. She was doing a great job, but today, some kid thought it would be neat to take one of the eggs home with them, so they could have their very own pet duck."

"What an enterprising kid," I said, dryly. "I guess that's one way to have the pet your parents won't allow." I could definitely empathise with that part. Less so the stealing bit.

"Fortunately, the child's mother realised that their little girl was keeping something warm in her hands before they left the zoo. The egg was returned and it seems to be fine, although Jemima doesn't want it back, as far as I can tell. It's been put in an incubator instead."

"I wonder how many eggs have made it out of the zoo that way?" I mused, thinking about how wayward children could be with little clue of the consequences. It was part of what being a child was about and it was definitely where a parent's experience came in.

"More than a few. The bog-standard eggs go missing all the time. We used to offer the first children in of the day a chance to go and collect them up to take home, but health and safety these days is all over that. Salmonella could get us sued, or something." She rolled her eyes, but kept on smiling. "Anyway… the kids still take them. But it's not often they get their hands anywhere near the broody birds. Well - not without being nipped for their trouble. She must have been seriously desperate for a pet duck!"

"I'm glad you got the egg back okay and Jemima is still going strong."

"You betcha! She's a great mother, that one. It'll be great when she has ducklings in tow. We lost a lot of ducks due to a disease that swept through them a while back." She looked forlorn remembering. "It was just one of those things that could happen to anyone at anytime. I was heartbroken, but it happened so quickly. When the vet came, he said there was nothing to be done." She perked up again. "That's why it'll be lovely to have a whole host of new characters! And we won't need to say goodbye to them either, like usual."

"Do the ducks usually go to other zoos?"

"A lot of the time, yes. Zoos have unfortunate incidents like the one we had. However, ducks aren't the most in-demand animal around. Sometimes there's a surplus. Then they get sold to private collectors." She raised her eyebrows at me. "What happens next is anyone's guess. I hope they have happy lives."

I nodded my agreement. It was sometimes difficult to find places for animals when it appeared no one wanted them. The best thing to do was reduce breeding to avoid unnecessary suffering for any 'leftover' animals.

It was only after Robyn had walked away to disentangle a screaming child from a very unhappy rabbit, and I'd returned to having my clothing eaten away by a goat, that I realised something significant. Eggs were easy to smuggle and very hard to keep track of. Instead of waiting around for a tiger litter to be born, perhaps I should be focusing on some of the other easy-to-smuggle zoo residents, who might otherwise have been overlooked. I mentally consulted my 'likely to be smuggled' animals list in my head, based off some probably flawed internet research, and decided that the reptile and amphibian department of the zoo was where I should switch my attentions.

With hindsight, I should have thought about it before. Way back when Auryn's father had been involved in smuggling animals to sell on the exotic pets blackmarket (and who knew? Perhaps to these very same smugglers) one of his favourite things to do had been to fudge the number of eggs sent and received. The penguins had suffered that blow but I thought (after my research) I was more likely to strike gold with turtles, terrapins, and snakes.

It was time for a change of tactics.

My phone rang in the middle of the afternoon when I was halfway between a goat and the child whose top it was trying to consume. The boy's father was shouting about how it was a designer t-shirt and had cost a bomb, but I was more interested in trying to stop the kid from being strangled by the particularly unyielding fabric. In the end, the kid lost his shirt to the goat, but lived to tell the tale. I was left nervously adjusting my wig to make sure it was still in place (and unconsumed) whilst fending off the father's demands for the zoo to pay for a replacement shirt.

The vast majority of parents and children who visited the pet zone were as polite, friendly, and respecting of the animals as could be, but unfortunately it was the bad ones who stuck in your mind. My phone ringing halfway through our heated discussion just made things worse... especially when I turned my back on the man and answered my phone. I was well aware that it might stick out as out of character for a new zookeeper to dare to be so rude to a customer, but I'd decided I wasn't going to be a doormat for any money.

"Hi Tiff," I said, feeling a wash of relief at hearing a familiar voice. I missed The Lucky Zoo and Avery. Even though we were within commuting distance of the zoo we were currently working in, our two zoos had barely had a five minute visit in the time we'd left. Everything had been running smoothly, but I was still drawn back there.

"What have you been sticking your nose into this time?" She didn't sound impressed.

I frowned. "I'm sorry?"

"Why are you poking around in my husband's affairs? You can't possibly suspect him of murder. What's your problem?"

I bit my lip to keep from saying that he was actually on

my list of possible suspects, given what I imagined about his past. "What does he think I've been doing?" I was genuinely curious. All I'd been able to do thus far was a few internet searches and asking people like Katya and...

Oh.

I'd asked Lowell.

"Someone told him you were inquiring about his past. Apparently, you think he's lying about being a detective, or some such nonsense. Honestly, Madi... I swear you see monsters lurking in every shadow. I know Alex. I love him. And I would appreciate it if you butt out."

"I just wanted to make sure he's the man you think he is. You don't deserve someone lying to you," I told her, giving up the pretence that I hadn't been looking into Alex. I had Lowell to thank for that.

"I know who he is just fine. I married him. Now, please, I cannot believe I'm even having to say this... but keep your nose out of other people's business!" And with that, she hung up.

I was left with the worrying idea that I might have just lost another friend. And I hadn't had that many to start with.

The only thing I could think of to make myself feel better was to go after the person responsible for getting me into this mess.

I found Lowell in the shed, staring at the video Joe had left for me with a glazed expression on his face. I didn't ask what he hoped to glean from it by watching it for the thousandth time.

"So much for 'you can trust me'," I said, announcing my presence with an attack.

He spun around on his chair. I noticed he didn't look at

all surprised to see me here. If anything, there was a smug air about him that hinted he'd orchestrated it all along.

"Your detective must be worried if he runs to tell his wife to get you to stop snooping at the first hint of your curiosity. If it were me, I'd have stayed quiet, knowing how it would look if I kicked up too much of a fuss."

I watched Lowell in silence for a few moments, trying to figure him out. Was he attempting to claim he'd been helping me? I wasn't going to play games with my ex-boyfriend. "Just who is Alex Gregory? And don't lie," I added - although it probably wouldn't make any difference at all.

"He's no one important," Lowell said with this infuriating half-shrug, all the while still looking up at Joe's video, like it was suddenly the most fascinating thing ever.

I ground my teeth together. "My best friend isn't talking to me because of you. You're going to have to do better than that." I walked over and spun the wheelie chair he was sitting on around to face me.

For a second, Lowell looked surprised by my strength. I shot him a look warning him that I was more than willing to use a little more, unless he started talking. Now.

He let out a long sigh and rested his hands on the back of his head, showing off some enviable biceps that had once made me feel all fuzzy inside. Now I surveyed him with cool indifference.

"It's a funny story. Alex is just like me, in a way. No - he's not using your friend to spy on anyone," he said before I bit his head off. "He never wanted a life with Intelligence. He started his career in the police force in the normal way... but it turned out he had quite the talent for violence. Nothing like wild aggression just... when he got into a scrape, he could get himself out of it pretty easily."

I thought about Alex's lean physique and the hardness

that lived behind his eyes and thought I could get on board with that.

"A skill like that gets you noticed by a few different kinds of people. Before I bet he even knew what was happening, he was picking up odd jobs. I'm sure he never thought he was doing anything illegal, but..." Lowell shrugged, meaning that Alex's jobs probably hadn't been exactly clean either. "Of course, it wasn't long before he got himself into trouble and good old British Intelligence stepped in and offered him an opportunity he couldn't refuse. He would work for them and they would make sure his police career wouldn't get ruined by the mistake he'd made. They came through. Look at where he is now, especially considering his age."

"What mistake?" I asked. I hadn't missed that little slip of information.

Lowell shrugged again. "I don't know. He picked the wrong side, I guess. Got himself into trouble. I only know him professionally, and I didn't know his real name."

"Right..." I said, not willing to believe every word out of Lowell's mouth. "What is he doing here?"

Lowell grinned. "That's the funny part of the story. After doing MI5's dirty work, he's managed to persuade them that he deserves a long break. A permanent one, I think. I don't know how he's managed it - don't ask me, I wish I knew - but all he wants to do is settle down in a quiet little town and start a new life."

I folded my arms. "And you want me to believe that, by pure chance, he chose Gigglesfield?"

Lowell's smile got wider. "No, of course not. He asked me if I knew anywhere quiet and sleepy - the kind of place where nothing ever happens. We were together in Brighton right around the time when we were all working at the zoo, and it just popped into my head to tell him to go there. To be honest, I thought he might go to Gigglesfield and then realise

I was pulling his leg when he found out you were here. But I guess I didn't think about him not being on the money laundering case. He wouldn't have known that trouble seems to follow you around like a bad smell." I glared at Lowell when he said that. Charming he was not. "Since then, you've had a few murders, haven't you? Again, I would have thought he'd pack up and leave after realising I'd been stringing him along, but I hadn't counted on him falling in love." For just a second, Lowell looked wistful.

"He really didn't know about the money laundering case?" I was still having a hard time trusting Lowell.

"No. He wasn't selected for it. I know that much, being on the team myself. Things are usually kept quiet concerning operations." He eyed me when he said it. "With that body turning up and our investigation, I don't envy Alex Gregory. He has to do his job whilst covering up the truth about exactly who we are and what we're investigating. He wanted a life and a career away from all of the drama. Instead, he's back in the middle of it."

"Are you sure he wouldn't have known who Joe was?" I pressed, trying to marry up the little that I knew.

Lowell frowned. "I couldn't say for certain, but he was fairly unrecognisable after the surgery, wasn't he?" He shook his head. "I don't know. What makes you have him pegged for the killer?" My ex-boyfriend still knew me fairly well.

"Joe recognised him," I confessed, figuring it was easier than concocting a lie that checked out. Anyway, Joe was dead, and Alex Gregory was supposedly retired from espionage.

Lowell's eyebrows shot up. "I did say he made a mistake that put him under the service's control. It sounds like you might have just found out what it was."

I felt my mouth move into a thin line. Alex Gregory had fallen in with the money launderers. I'd hoped for answers, but instead I was left with a fresh can of worms. If I believed Lowell's claim that Alex was retired from all things MI5, that was one part solved, but the knowledge that he'd probably worked for Joe's colleagues in the past didn't exactly make him look like a shining beacon of innocence. And I could definitely see that he'd had the opportunity, and potentially a motive, to murder Joe. Had Detective Gregory figured out my marketing and PR guru's real identity at the same time Joe had recognised him? Unfortunately, I had to consider that it was possible. It was very possible.

"I'm sorry I did it now. It was selfish. I put Alex in your path to get back at you for not trusting me. I guess I knew that if anything did happen, he'd be sure to give you a hard time. I shouldn't have done it."

I looked at Lowell in surprise for a moment, at a loss for what to say. "He makes my best friend very happy," was what I settled for in the end. "I just hope…" I left it hanging. I just hoped that everything Lowell had told me was the truth and not a carefully selected part of it, and I hoped that Alex Gregory genuinely did love my best friend and want nothing to do with MI5. Most of all, I hoped that somehow the truth would come out in the best possible way and no hearts or friendships would be broken by it.

"How are you getting on?" I asked, inclining my head towards the paused video on screen.

"Saying we've hit a dead end doesn't seem to quite cover it. We've got nothing. I've been scouring this video for any hints of anything, but I'm starting to think you're right. Your guy made it for you in order to impart some last minute advice on how to sort out pastoral affairs. There's nothing big in it."

I decided to overlook Lowell's dig at what he considered to be my petty problems. We were making progress at being civil to one another and I was trying to maintain it. "What about my death threat?"

"Nothing on that either. You're still alive, so that's something."

"Indeed it is," I said, my voice heavy with sarcasm.

Lowell smirked, but not unkindly. "No progress on your animal smugglers?"

I shook my head. I'd figured out that I might be looking in the wrong places for the bad guys, but that was still all just hypothetical. I didn't have any concrete evidence at all to suggest that smuggling was even taking place at Corbyn Manor.

"What are these money launderers really like? Are they actually that bad?" It had been a question that had bugged me for ages. British Intelligence wanted to lock them up and throw away the key, which automatically made you believe they must have a good reason for it. But Joe's words were making me want to delve deeper. *One person's freedom fighter is another's terrorist*, I remembered and wondered if there was something similar happening here.

Lowell looked back at the screen with thought lining his face. He, too, must be thinking of the video. After all - he'd watched the darn thing enough times. "It's complicated. I don't know all there is to know. At the heart of it, I'm a mercenary - just like your detective friend. I do what I'm told and get my pay-check." My heart stung a little when he said it so matter-of-factly, and apparently without a thought about who he was saying it to. "I'm sure they might spin you any number of lines about their virtue and their good causes, whilst spouting about corrupt governments, but they have broken the law many, many times. And they have done terrible things."

When it comes to war, both sides are guilty, I silently thought to myself.

"Don't trust any of them, Madi," he implored.

"They're not the ones who've broken my trust," I told him, before turning to walk out of the shed.

He caught me before I'd taken two steps. His hand was firm on my upper arm. When I turned around he was looking down at me, just a ruler's distance away. "Don't make the same mistake others have made."

I felt my mouth harden into a determined line. "I won't," I promised him, before brushing him off and walking out of the shed unhindered. I kept my back turned to him so he couldn't see the pink in my cheeks where, just for a moment, I'd been reminded of our past in a far too vivid way. Beyond the physical attraction that had been - and apparently glimmers of still remained - our entire conversation was just another reminder of why Lowell and I would never have worked out. He could never be upfront with me and I resented him for it. I was glad that I'd ended things when I had and, in spite of that shine in Lowell's eyes, there was zero chance of us making a return to the past. I was in love, married, and ready for my happily ever after.

My phone rang as I was stalking back towards the pet zone. I answered it without looking.

"What?" I barked, probably forever estranging the person on the other end.

"Hi Madi. It's Drew James here. I just wanted you to know how sorry I am for everything that happened. I realise now how wrong it was, and I was just as horrified as anyone to discover who was responsible for the deaths of my fellow estate agents."

"What do you want? And how did you get my number?!" I wasn't in the mood for batting around pleasantries with a criminal I'd helped to catch. Even before then, I'd never particularly got on with Drew James. Mostly because he'd decided my relationship with Auryn was some sort of challenge to overcome.

"It's about your zoo. Remember when I said I knew something about the property? And I got your number from Sophia's files."

"Right. Well, please forget you ever had it," I said and hung up. Of all the nerve! I had no idea at all why a dog stealer like Drew would think I'd ever in a million years want to chat property with him. It was complete madness. I blocked his number and made a mental note to regard all future unknown number calls with extreme suspicion.

According to MI5, I'd done enough fraternising with criminals already to last a lifetime.

7

THE CULT OF COMMON SENSE

L ife at Corbyn Manor was not turning out the way I'd hoped. One and a half weeks in, with Halloween steadily approaching, the only thing scary was how low my mood was. An unknowing observer would have questioned my negative outlook. The pet zone was looking better than ever. The rabbit problem had been solved, and many of the changes Robyn had been lobbying for had been granted - so much so that she'd started calling me her lucky charm and seemed convinced that I must be a master of negotiation. The truth was, I was doing the job I'd been employed to do, and those high up enough in the zoo to make a difference were so unnerved by the presence of the Secret Service and my part in it, they were willing to jump to whatever I said.

Underneath it all, I knew I was failing. Auryn and I had done everything we could to assimilate into the zoo's staff - in spite of the unwelcome crowd making newcomers even less popular than normal. The problem was, people tended to stick to their cliques. Harry the big cat keeper was the only one un-snobby enough to say hello to me, a lowly pet zookeeper, but, with the exception of Rowena, the reptile and amphibian keepers were even less friendly.

The way things were going, Auryn and I weren't going to crack the smuggling ring. To make matters worse, the tight-knit groups made it next to impossible to come up with a proper review. I was used to working with keepers, not as a spy against them.

I was nearly at my wits end when I found the torn-up piece of paper. With the blessed gift of hindsight, I should have known it was too obvious and too much like a Nancy Drew clue. But I was so desperate I fell for it, hook, line, and sinker.

I was doing my best to hang around the building where newborn animals and incubators were kept. I'd managed to stay there on the pretence of checking in on the duck eggs that were currently incubating (Jemima's friends weren't all as dedicated as she was). Whenever I could, I would creep around the building trying to find any trace of the alleged smuggling operation. I don't know what I'd hoped to find, but the piece of paper in the bin seemed to fit the bill.

I'd reasoned that anyone tearing something up might have something to hide. Also, the note had looked handwritten...well, anyway... I was really desperate.

Heather and Millstone Park 8pm Tuesday

That was what the note said when I'd pieced it together. I'd quickly extracted myself from the gloomy, heat-lamp lit reptiles and amphibians hatching ground and had retreated to research just what it meant. All I knew was that today was Monday. This note could mean nothing. It could even refer to last Tuesday, or have absolutely nothing to do with animal smuggling, but I was running low on options. Any lead was good enough for me.

I walked back down the corridor towards the exit. I wouldn't have noticed the shadow in the records room had they not dropped a file on the floor and sworn. I froze in the doorway. Had I just happened upon the very thing I'd been looking for all the time I'd been here? Was this one of the guilty culprits editing the records of their animals?

The shadow turned round and I recognised the blank features and poorly fitting suit.

"Mr Flannigan, what are you doing here?"

"I could ask the same of you. It's a little late to still be here, isn't it?"

The zoo had closed four hours ago, so he wasn't wrong.

"I was checking in on some of the incubators. Some ducks are hatching soon."

Flannigan arched his eyebrows. "I know you're not inclined to tell me the truth, but we are Britain's best. I've watched you come in here for several days in a row. No other zookeepers have put in so much work. Perhaps it's your dedication that has won you so many accolades, but... I think it's something else. It wouldn't have anything to do with the animal smugglers believed to be operating out of here, would it?"

I tried to show neither surprise nor prior knowledge. "What were you hoping to find in those records?" I asked, equally sure that he'd been in the middle of something shady when he'd dropped that file.

We faced each other down for a moment, both eyeing the other with thinly veiled suspicion.

"How about a truce?" Flannigan suggested. "I'll tell you, if you'll tell me. You go first."

Some part of me wanted to accuse him of trying to get me to talk whilst he remained silent. After all - he was the spy, and the one who was supposed to keep secrets from everyone else. In the end, I decided to break the habit of a lifetime and throw him a bone. Otherwise, I had this nasty feeling he'd start following me even more closely. "I think that some of the staff at this zoo may be implicated in an animal smuggling operation."

Flannigan smirked. "Just as I suspected. What are they doing? Selling off a few alligators for handbags?"

"Shipping them out of the UK to foreign markets," I replied, incensed into replying. "What were you doing looking through those records?"

Flannigan frowned for a second, before his expression cleared. "That's what this is all about, isn't it? That's why you're really here. You've made all of us follow you here to this ridiculous plastic amusement park, so you can save a few animals and feel good about yourself."

I bit my tongue to keep from saying that it was hardly 'a few animals', but I didn't exactly hold all the facts, did I? In truth, I still had yet to find a shred of proof beyond a wayward lynx that anything untoward had happened at all.

"No… it's worse than that. This all ties in with the death of your employee somehow, doesn't it?" He looked at me and must have read that he was on the right path. "His body was found in a lynx enclosure. So… it was to do with animal smuggling, and you thought you'd keep that from us."

"It wasn't anything to do with animal smuggling. That's just what someone wanted us to think," I patiently explained, before elaborating on that theory.

By the time I'd finished, Flannigan looked more unimpressed than ever. "I could have you arrested and taken in for questioning. You can't withhold evidence like this!"

I shrugged. "I thought I was too busy acting as bait for you to catch whoever sent me that death threat." We both knew it was true. MI5 were hoping that the person who thought I knew too much would follow up on their little threat and try to finish the job. I wasn't too certain that MI5 wouldn't just sit back and let it happen... just to make sure they had the right man.

Flannigan ground his teeth for a moment. "Aside from your own petty prejudices... why did you keep this knowledge to yourself?"

I took a deep breath and explained how there wasn't exactly any evidence to share. I wasn't so certain that all of this hadn't been a figment of our imagination. Or worse - some kind of game Joe had been playing in order to manipulate me, before someone had killed him in a way that, by pure chance, had made it look like it had been to do with animal smugglers.

I didn't buy it. It was too unlikely. Someone had known that we were investigating. I shook my head to clear it. I was going round in circles, chasing my tail, and the man in front of me wasn't helping.

"How about you tell me why you're sneaking around?" I said, fed up with playing Flannigan's game.

He examined his manicured fingernails. "If you must know, I was doing background checks. You should never underestimate the people around you or believe you know who they are. We've run preliminaries on everyone, of course. But the people we're after are good. I wanted to look through the personal employment records at the zoo."

I raised my eyebrows. "Surely you'd have access to that?"

He shook his head, a wan smile on his face. "I'm afraid not. Things aren't the way they appear in films and TV shows. You can't just delve into someone's private records without having a genuine reason to suspect them."

I shot him a disbelieving look. They'd delved deep enough into my own affairs without asking permission or having any reason to suspect that I was up to no good. I wasn't convinced by what I was being told, but I couldn't be bothered to pursue it. All I really wanted to do was get out of Flannigan's company.

I should have been paying more attention.

"If there really is a group of smugglers who are shipping things - anything - out of the UK illegally on such a large scale, and who may have even been driven to murder, it's something MI5 should be working on," he informed me.

"Of course," I said, able to agree on that much. I wasn't really dead against authority and so keen to fling myself in the path of danger. "Unfortunately, until we find evidence to prove that all of this isn't just a tall tale, there's nothing anyone else can do. Well - apart from keeping quiet about it." I looked meaningfully at the man opposite me, wondering if I should even be bothering to ask.

After a moment's pause he nodded. "You've given me enough reason to believe that your man wasn't murdered by the smugglers, and it is plausible that the entire thing is a farce. We'll keep looking for the gang of high-level criminals who are most likely to blame for the murder and the threats made against you. I'm willing to keep this under my hat."

"Thanks for your discretion," I said, somewhat sarcastically if truth be told. Flannigan and I would never be friends.

"If you ask me, whoever did murder the man you knew as Joe Harvey was aware of your investigation. That means they probably know exactly what you're up to right now. Think about that," he said, before slipping out of the room and into the night.

The thought had crossed my mind many a time before, but I did think about it - more now than ever. And I also wondered just who held all the cards... and if they were playing with me, even now.

The phone ringing woke me up the next morning. I blinked blearily and was just able to make out Georgina's name on the screen.

"Hi," I said, trying to make my mind catch up with my mouth. It was early, that was for sure, but I wasn't entirely surprised to discover that the high-flying lawyer was awake and sounding peppy. I should have been able to guess she was a morning person.

"Our little club's made the front page. Apparently, you're starting a women-only cult." She made a 'tsk tsk' noise of disapproval.

I groaned. Who the heck had told the press about the club we were starting?

"Before you ask, of course I found out who told the press. I'm not a lawyer for nothing. I don't think we can apportion any blame though. Annemarie Wickington told her husband as soon as she said yes to our club. He pulled some strings and got the press to spin it that way."

"I doubt he needed to pull many strings," I said, dryly. I was hardly the media's darling right now.

"Well, I think it's brilliant," Georgina stated, surprising the heck out of me. "Before you protest, just remember that we need all the publicity we can get. And the more ridiculous we look, the better! We're supposed to be setting up as the female equivalent of their jumped-up boys' club. If the media paints us as some man-hating cult, it won't be too hard to convince them that the other side is just as bad. With a bit of luck, we'll both be laughed out of town."

"I suppose you're right," I said, struggling to wrap my head around the chess game that was taking place at this early hour.

"I know I am. Anyway, looking forward to our meeting tomorrow! Everything is going swimmingly so far. Do you know, it's only six in the morning, but the other early birds in town have already messaged me asking what the club is all about? When I explain, they all want to join." She hesitated. "They can join, can't they?"

"Yes, of course." We weren't trying to be anything like as exclusive as the Lords of the Downs. That was the whole point. They excluded so many people, whilst allowing a powerful few to have a say over everyone.

"I've had men ask to join, too. I did say no to them, but I felt mean doing it. It stops being a man-hating cult if we let them in, and we couldn't have that. It might damage our press." I wasn't sure if she was being sarcastic or serious at this point. "Anyway, must dash! Lots of tax evaders to help out," she said cheerfully, before hanging up.

I was left wondering whether she'd genuinely meant 'help out'. I decided she probably had.

Even as I lay back on the pillow to try to salvage another hour of sleep I felt a smile spreading across my face. Nigel Wickington had gone to the press for help. The Lords of the Downs were rattled.

Unfortunately, before I could share the clue I'd found in the incubation room with Auryn, he informed me that there was a Lords of the Downs meeting this evening. According to my husband, it was some sort of emergency that he couldn't possibly miss. I'd bitten my tongue for a full minute, wondering whether it would be better to warn him or not - considering that the club might think we were conspiring together. I didn't want Auryn to be tarred with the same brush. But secrets were something we'd promised never to keep from one another.

"You've started a cult?" he said when I'd finished. I hadn't explained very well.

"No, a club. It's just like your club, but for successful women." I didn't bother to elaborate that our definition of 'successful' was a lot looser than the Lords of the Downs'. We took all comers.

"In order to stop a club you claim is a ridiculous 'men-only' elitist invention, you create a similar club." Auryn didn't look impressed.

"Exactly. The press already hate us." I showed him the online news reports all claiming that I was some kind of cult leader. "Apparently, we have Nigel Wickington to thank for the early publicity. The old sweetheart."

Auryn was frowning at me. "You're pleased? It makes you sound ridiculous."

"Which is a good thing," I said and explained why - courtesy of Georgina's reasoning.

By the end of it, Auryn looked less confused, but not entirely convinced. "There'll be reprisals." He gulped. "I think I may be lynched tonight…"

"That's why I thought it was only fair to warn you. There's safety in numbers and trust me… we've got the numbers." Wealth only went so far when you had a select few holding it. It sounded like a bad political slogan, but we were many, and they were few. We may not all be rich (although admittedly, the group leaders weren't too hard-up) but there were enough of us to make a difference, and hopefully put a stop to the Lords of the Downs holding all local businesses in a thrall.

"Next you'll be holding your own local business awards night. There aren't enough dates on the calendar," Auryn complained, but I could tell he wasn't peeved anymore. He wanted an end to the reign of the club he was a member of as much as anyone.

"I don't think that will be our style. I know we're competing in terms of name and goals, but even though this is all set up to be a thorn in our rivals' sides, I think it would be nice if we contributed something to the community rather than deeming who should have their success stripped from them."

"Okay," he said, nodding his head. "As schemes go, I suppose it's better than nothing."

"Thanks a lot," I replied, showing him my best frown face.

He laughed and patted me on the head, knowing I hated it. "I'm sure your club will do great. I'm sorry. I'm just projecting my own worries onto you. I already said I'd go tonight. If I back out now, it will look like I'm a traitor…" He winced at his own words. "To tell the truth, I wish I'd come up with your idea. But… being a women-only club does make more sense. It makes a better point. Rather than a bitter ex-member forming their own club." He gave a self-deprecating smile.

"There's something else you need to know…" I said and told him about the clue I'd found in the bin last night. To my surprise, Auryn was remarkably positive about it. However, when I'd reminded him that he was due at a club meeting tonight, he'd been less cheerful.

"There's no one you can ask to go with you, is there?" he said, gloomily.

"I'm not about to ask Mr Flannigan," I replied, hoping to brighten the mood.

When Auryn looked thoughtful for a moment, I nearly fell out of my chair.

"What about Lowell?" he asked.

"What about him?" I said, not thrilled to be hearing the name of my ex uttered by my husband like it was a good idea.

"You told me that Katya told him about what we were up to. He could act as protection." When he saw my face he continued: "We've got to take whatever allies we can get."

"I don't trust him. He's the reason why Tiff isn't talking to me!" I still hadn't managed to patch things up with my best friend.

"He's also the reason why Gigglesfield police force landed such an excellent and scrupulous detective. He may have a past he's unwilling to open up about, but I still think he's a good man. Tiff will come round, too. Once everything is out in the open - in it's own time - I think everything will be as it always has been."

I hoped that this rather philosophical view would prove to be true, but I wasn't convinced that everything didn't look like a big fat mess right now.

"Ask Lowell," Auryn repeated.

"I can go by myself," I countered. "I'll wear my disguise. If anyone from the zoo sees me, I'll act like it's some big coincidence." It sounded weak even to my own ears. I'd looked up the park in question. It was miles from the zoo in some back of beyond neighbourhood. Whilst it definitely fitted my idea of a sketchy secret rendezvous location, it was less easy to explain away my presence if caught. "I can look after myself."

Auryn shot me a look that was supposed to remind me of all the times I'd come oh-so-close to being knocked out of the race of life for good. I held my ground. This was about principles!

Auryn sighed. "You know you don't need my permission to do anything. We're partners, not prisoners to one another. But... it would make me happy if you were to take someone with you. I only suggested Lowell because, although untrustworthy in terms of being upfront and honest, he doesn't strike me as a traitor. In fact, his silence with you probably proves his loyalty to his cause over anything."

"I suppose..." I grudgingly allowed. I'd been building my case for Lowell being the traitor in my head, but I was stacking a poorly built house of cards. "But he was someone who knew about the animal smuggling before Joe's death. Katya told him. That means he could have been the one who killed him and framed him that way! He's also been involved with smugglers before. He could have signed on to the dark side back then." I knew I was jumping at shadows, but wasn't it better to jump than to stand around and wait for the hammer to fall?

"If that's true, if I were you, I'd keep him where you can see him. You know what they say about your enemies…"

"I don't think *they* are talking about murderers when they say that. Do you really want me hanging out with someone who might have murdered a person?"

"Of course I don't… but I don't think he'll murder you."

I looked up into Auryn's grey eyes and saw that he knew as well as I did that Lowell still held onto something of mine - no matter how over I knew we were. "Okay. I'll ask him. But I'll do it last minute, so he can't tip anyone off. And if he says no…" I thought about it. "I won't let him say no," I decided, realising that it was all or nothing. If I told Lowell and went without him, he could be on the phone the minute I left.

"Come back safe," Auryn said, pulling me in close.

"You too," I told him, thinking of his club meeting.

I wasn't sure who was in more danger.

The first bite of winter was in the air when Lowell and I crept into the park. Fortunately, most of the bushes were evergreens, so there was plenty of cover. Unfortunately, it was autumn, so there were a whole lot of crunchy leaves on the ground. It was hardly the ideal spy mission.

"You look ridiculous," Lowell hissed as we sneaked from bush to bush. He had to bend double, but I barely needed to stoop. Sometimes there were advantages to being vertically challenged.

"Well sorr-ee for not shopping at Spys 'R' Us fashion store." I'd worn black tonight because black was what you wore when you needed to get some sneaking done, right? However, I'd discovered that after a summer clear-out I was running pretty short on black clothes. I liked a splash of colour when I was out of my zoo uniform. All I'd been able to find was a black cat costume stuffed at the bottom of the wardrobe. It was a relic from a Halloween so long past I'd been surprised to find it in the things I'd taken from my old place. I'd grabbed it and had only discovered how bad it looked when I'd poured myself into it, before hitting the road with a reluctant Lowell.

Whilst I didn't take kindly to fashion critiques, I did admit that the tail was a bit of a hindrance.

"If anyone catches us, don't let them take me alive. I'll never live it down," Lowell sniped.

I was about to do some sniping back, but a curious expression of surprise came over Lowell's face. Suddenly, he was falling. Right on top of me.

After ascertaining that none of my ribs had been broken, I managed to crawl out from beneath Lowell's bulk. Some-where along the way, I lost the tail I'd been unable to detach from the costume. My wig didn't make it out either.

All in all, it must have made pretty amusing viewing for the person watching my every move.

"Madigan Amos. It has been a while," a voice drawled.

I pushed myself up off of my stomach, disentangling my legs from beneath Lowell's inert form. For a moment, I looked back at him with dread. The fluffy tip of a tranquil-liser dart stuck out from his back, reassuring me that he was probably okay.

Unless they'd used a dart meant for an elephant.

I turned back to face the person to blame.

It took me a few moments to recognise her. After all, I'd only met her once before, and I'd been giddy with daydreams about my comic's success at the time.

Leona Dresden from Rock and Roll Publishing - my first and very fake publishing company I'd signed a deal with - was standing in front of me.

To my surprise, she looked exactly the same as she had when I'd last seen her.

"I don't go in for any of that surgery nonsense," she said, accurately reading the confusion on my face. "I prefer to disappear rather than flaunt myself unnecessarily close to the boiling pot." She regarded me with unconcealed disdain.

"What do you want?" I asked, regretting ever having snooped around and trusted such a convenient clue, left lying in a wastepaper basket.

"I want to know what dear departed Jordan told you before he met with such an unfortunate end," she said, her eyes bright and terrifying. I noticed she was using the name he'd used when posing as a literary agent.

"What he told me about what?"

"Us. Our operation. I could see he had a soft spot for you from the very first. I also know he's got a flair for drama, and after the disappearing act he pulled, I have no doubt he'd have done everything he could to rat us out, if he were killed under suspicious circumstances." She shook her head. "It seems obvious now. He thought his best way to escape was to stay with you, probably thinking it would be the last place we'd look. Really, he was blinded by his feelings. I should have known he'd slip the net as soon as he got fixed. I don't even know what he looked like in the end."

I was struck by the cruel memory of the mess that had been all that remained of Joe's face. "He was telling the truth when he said he wanted to get out of his underworld life?"

Leona rolled her eyes. "Clearly. Why else would he be skulking in the shadows working for someone like you. It's not as if he was hard-up for money. Everything was for you." She shot me a disgusted look. "I hope you're happy. Whatever you had him tangling with, it got him killed."

"Are you trying to convince me that you're not the ones responsible for killing him?"

"We had nothing to do with it. We were looking, of course, but we couldn't find him. Jordan knew the best surgeons and he also knew how to pay them to shut-up. It's a code of honour. They won't talk, no matter what you do, and you can't do much or they won't help you next time you need it." She shook her head. "It might make sense from a business point of view, but it's a headache. Jordan vanished on the same day I dissolved our publishing house operations." Her lip curled up. "You were supposed to go down with the ship, by the way."

I shrugged. I'd known that much. Leona's signature had been on the contract note that had been found on Joe's body. I could only assume that Joe had managed to go behind her back on that front, too. He'd engineered it so that I was free to sign with another publisher, without having to face the prospect of a legal battle against an opponent who'd vanished off the face of the earth. I had, however, believed that the contract note had been left as a message from Leona and her crew - sort of like a calling card.

"Would you have killed him if you'd found him?" I asked, remembering a time when I'd overheard Leona and my ex-literary agent arguing. There hadn't been any love lost between them then, and I knew that surprising things could drive people to murder.

"No. We'd have brought him back into the fold. He'd have been punished, but he was worth the trouble." She eyed me speculatively. "You probably know that if he was working for you. You can't just walk away from our operation. Once you're in, you're in for life." *Now where have I heard that before?* I sarcastically thought, knowing that MI5 tended to operate along the same guidelines. That's what made me so suspicious of Alex Gregory's theoretical break from them. I wasn't convinced that it was possible.

Leona pointedly hefted the tranquilliser gun on her shoulder, reminding me who was in charge here. "I believe I was the one asking you the questions. What did he tell you about us?"

"Nothing. Well - next to nothing," I said, somehow knowing it wasn't the answer she wanted, even though it was the truth. "He sent a video to me after his death." Leona rolled her eyes when I told her that. "It didn't say anything about you, or your... group." I wasn't sure how to describe the money launderers. "All he said was for me to try to understand that things aren't as black and white as they're painted. I think he wanted me to believe you're not everything they say you are. Perhaps you're even doing some good things." I shrugged. I hadn't managed to get beyond that.

"We're hardly philanthropists." Leona watched me with eyes that were able to see right through to everything I might be holding back. "Are you going to stick with your story?"

I nodded. It was the truth.

She shook her head like I was crazy. "Well... that completely clears up why you're dragging MI5 around with you as a personal escort." Sarcasm didn't really cover it.

"Oh. Him," I said, remembering that Lowell was probably quite an obvious double agent. He'd snagged a job working for the publishing company. It would make sense that Leona would remember his face and be able to put two and two together as easy as pie.

"He wouldn't be sticking to you like glue if he weren't here for us. And don't say it's to do with the animal smuggling you're snooping around. They don't care about that. They care about money."

I shrugged. "I got a tip-off about this park being a meeting place for that kind of thing. That's why I'm here - although, it's pretty clear that it was just a trick." Boy, did I feel stupid.

A flash of concern crossed Leona's face for a fraction of a second before it lapsed back into being expressionless. "What do you know?"

"Nothing," I said, raising my hands when she lifted the gun threateningly, meaning to use it as a club. "I don't know anything. There's no reason to kill me. What do you think I should know?! Clearly it's something important enough to send via newspaper clippings and Pritt Stick."

Leona's face definitely clouded with confusion now.

"The death threat you sent," I prompted. This was getting weirder by the second.

"I didn't send you any threat." She looked thoughtful for a moment. "Perhaps this does have something to do with those second-rate thieves." She shook her head, apparently drawing a conclusion that contradicted whatever theory she'd been pulling together in her mind. "MI5 are following you like vultures. You know something." She took a step closer. "If you crack to them first…" I was free to fill in the blanks any way I chose. I assumed it wouldn't be tea and cake.

"How did you know to come here tonight?" I asked, realising that what I thought I knew, and what Leona thought I knew were two completely different things. And I thought I was beginning to see that both of us were being moved around the board

"I was in the area. It's a trade secret." she said, her cloudy expression clearing and her eyes glowing more dangerously than ever. I noticed that she fiddled with something in her pocket as she said it. It dropped onto the grass. She quickly bent and collected the hi-tech looking gadget, but not before I'd seen it. "I don't know what Joe ever saw in you," she said and then took off, slipping back between the bushes and vanishing from sight and sound.

I was left alone with an unconscious man who weighed twice as much as I did, and the worrisome feeling that the worst was yet to come.

Voices were approaching down the narrow path that wound through the park. I crouched down in the bushes and then realised that Lowell's inert form was all too visible lying out on the grass. Too late, I realised that camouflage would have been a better choice than midnight black.

With the silentest of sighs, I set to work trying to haul Lowell back under cover in a suitably quiet and subtle way. Somehow, I managed it just in time. As soon as he was under cover, two silhouetted figures walked around the corner on their way through the park.

"Nothing so far," the one on the left grunted. I held my breath, trying to keep my puffing and panting at bay. I did my fair share of heavy lifting at the zoo, but there was definitely a limit to my weightlifting abilities. When Lowell woke up, I was sure he'd have his fair share of bruises to show for my methods. Just so long as he actually woke up...

The moon was a bright semi-circle in the sky. As I watched whilst trying to keep my breathing silent I saw it reflect off something metal.

Both of the figures were carrying guns.

"They must have figured it out," the other voice came back.

"We won't get paid."

The other silhouette shrugged. "What do you want to do? Go through every tree, bush, and clump of daisies? We were told it would be a cinch. There's no one here, Grant. We'll tell them it was a bust and get paid for our time at least."

There was some grumbling on the other side, but a second later the footsteps went away, leaving me to sink back down on top of Lowell and take in all that I'd heard.

The clue had been fake after all. Someone had set me up! But not just me, I realised, remembering Leona's hi-tech looking device. Had she tracked us here, or had she been tipped off, too? Or had she tracked us and then herself been tracked? These men could have been gunning for both of us.

Someone was definitely playing me for a fool. And if I played their game for much longer, I would be dead.

8

CONVENIENT JUSTICE

The next morning, I woke up with a start. The memory of last night was still etched in my brain and the figure silhouetted against the window did nothing to quell those memories.

"Lowell?" I said, old memories being stirred up. By my side, Auryn continued to sleep.

"Luke, remember?" he said, good-naturedly. "But you can call me whatever you like. Thanks for helping me out last night."

I nodded. After the two would-be assassins had left, I'd waited a long and patient time in the bushes with Lowell, before I'd been able to bring him round enough that we'd struggled back to my car. When the men with guns had walked past our hiding place, I'd been glad I'd taken the time to park far away from the park and watching eyes, but on the long walk back, I'd lived to regret it.

I'd driven back to the house and installed Lowell on the sofa. I hadn't a clue where he was staying at the moment and honestly, I didn't think I wanted to know too much about it, but I couldn't have just left him.

"What happened, by the way?" A sheepish look came across Lowell's face.

"You were shot with a tranquilliser dart. Leona Dresden put in an appearance, and then a couple of men with guns strolled by hoping to catch us. If they'd done their jobs properly, we wouldn't be having this conversation this morning."

Lowell's face darkened. "After you explained how you found your so-called lead, I thought it was a trap. I was fool enough to think that I could handle it." He looked thoughtful for a moment. "So... it's your old publisher who's behind all of this. We've never been able to get close to her."

"She got close enough to you to put the dart in your back. But it's not her. I think she might have been manipulated the same way we were. Or perhaps it was just an unlucky coincidence." I remembered Leona's gadget and her casual mention that she'd been in the area. Was it just chance that the smugglers had picked a neighbourhood convenient for Leona when they'd dropped the clue about their secret meeting? But if it had been pre-planned, I wouldn't want to be the one who'd gone up against Leona Dresden and had let her get away alive. The mastermind behind it must either be a fool, or very, very clever indeed. Which it was remained to be seen.

"I don't believe in coincidences anymore," Lowell said, sounding like an actor in a bad thriller due to the drawl he'd developed as a last remaining side-effect from the dart.

"By the way... I think Leona was somehow tracking us. You should probably look into that. Maybe it's how they knew you were coming when you tried to bust them last time."

"That shouldn't be possible. We use every method on the market, and off it, to make ourselves untraceable. You can't just bug us." He cast a look in Auryn's direction before relaxing when he ascertained that he was still sleeping soundly.

I inclined my head to show we probably shouldn't be having this conversation here.

Thirty seconds later, now in the kitchen, we continued our discussion, but without getting anywhere. Lowell believed that Leona had drugged him and then when I had refused to play ball, she'd left us to the mercy of the hitmen she'd sent out earlier. I, on the other hand, was torn between the animal smugglers knowing we were onto them and acting accordingly... or, the old double-agent theory was certainly looking more plausible than ever. Who else would have been able to see the big picture and plant a clue for me and a local meet-up for Leona? Once more, I ran through my mental list of suspects for that role. And once more, I wasn't able to reduce it. Leona had drugged Lowell, but she hadn't killed him - even though she'd had every opportunity and knew he was the enemy. Either she was a philanthropist after all, or she'd gone easy on my ex-boyfriend for a good reason.

I regarded Lowell with care and he watched me back with the same guardedness.

"You should probably go," I said.

"You told him, didn't you?" he asked back at nearly the same moment.

I knew what he was asking. He was asking if I'd told Auryn the truth, even though I'd been bound not to do so. I didn't trust Lowell, and I didn't trust myself for telling a lie, so I said nothing.

My ex-boyfriend gave me one final unreadable look before turning and walking towards the front door.

"No!" I shouted before he could wrench it open.

He turned back to me with astonishment on his face.

"The press are out there. Go out through the woods." For a second, I felt a little bad for ruining his big dramatic exit, but the last thing I needed was the media claiming I had strange men staying the night and leaving in the early hours of the morning - especially when I had no doubt that someone would recognise Lowell from our past time together.

"Right. Of course," he said and slunk past out of the back-door and away down the garden.

I watched him go and despaired over what a waste of time last night had been. A deadly waste of time.

Gloria from LightStrike Publishing House called me before work was due to begin at the zoo that day. After surreptitious glances all round, I found a quiet corner and accepted the call.

"How is everything?" I asked even before we'd finished exchanging the usual pleasantries. The last time we'd spoken, Gloria had been concerned that the legal document found on Joe Harvey's person when he'd been murdered could affect our publishing contract.

"Oh, that's all fine. I had the legal team look into it and your dissolved contract was perfectly legal and at a later date to the document that was found. I wonder where this second document even came from! I'd hazard a guess that, for whatever reason, your old publishing company wanted to play hardball with you. What on earth did you do to rub them up the wrong way?" She meant it jokingly, but I grimaced. If only she knew the half of it!

"What can I say? I'm clearly a diva," I replied, equally unseriously.

"Anyway, I was just calling to let you know that we're all back on track here. Preorders are still going very well indeed. However..." She cleared her throat and I sensed that something less cheery was coming. "...you might want to consider your reputation. I know that once fame strikes, it's easy to take a lot of the opportunities that come your way, but not all of them are good decisions. Sometimes, you have to wonder why people are offering you these so-called opportunities and consider the long-term effect it might have on your career."

"I'm not starting a cult," I told her flatly, knowing exactly what she was tiptoeing around.

"Cult is such a strong word. I'm sure it's nothing of the sort. But even so..." She was trying to be soothing whilst definitely implying I'd joined a cult.

"It's a club for local businesswomen. There's already an equivalent club for the men, and they have rather a lot of influence with the locals. We all banded together and thought it was about time someone pushed them off their high horses, which was why we formed the club. However, our rivals haven't taken to the idea in the best of spirits." Auryn could attest to that after the grilling he'd told me he'd received the previous evening after he'd woken up this morning. They'd wanted to know exactly what we were planning, but I'd deliberately kept Auryn out of the loop. He'd been able to tell them absolutely nothing with a completely clear conscience. "They've fed a line to the media, and the media has lapped it up."

"I see," Gloria said, sounding relieved. I'd finally managed to convince her that I hadn't gone round the bend. "The other stuff they're saying isn't nice either, is it? I know it's not your fault, but it would be lovely if we could turn it around. You know what they say, today's papers are tomorrow's chip wrappers."

I made some sound of agreement, whilst privately thinking that in the past that may have been the case, but in this age of the internet, nothing truly disappeared once it was out there. "I wish there was something I could do to make this go away, but I'm flummoxed." I said it to show willing, but really, I had bigger fish to fry. Worrying about my bad publicity seemed silly when you compared it to nearly being shot last night.

"The press are fickle friends. I'm sure you'll get them onside again. All you need is one heroic act or obvious good deed, and they'll be fawning over you before you can say 'giving to charity'."

For a moment, I was treated to an interesting perspective on what it was like to be a celebrity, and worse - care about it. Instead of being guided by a moral compass, you were guided by media coverage and how certain acts would make you look. Got papped going nuts at the guy behind the burger stand? Bad. Get papped bringing coffee to a homeless person - you're a saint! Even then, celebrities were bitten when people asked them why they hadn't done more with their many millions. It was hard being on show all the time, and it wasn't something I wanted to continue forever.

"Hey… you know your employee who died? It would be brilliant if you could figure out who did it and bring them to justice. You've done that before, right?" Someone had been following the media reports, I realised. I supposed I should be grateful that Gloria had read the more favourable ones, as opposed to the ones that hinted I was a serial killer travelling the country under the guise of working as a zoo consultant.

"I'll do my best," I told her in order to keep her happy.

"Excellent! There's always a silver-lining to these things, isn't there?" Gloria said, before ringing off. I did some eyebrow raising over her trivialisation of death before shrugging it off. Gloria was a businesswoman first and foremost. She thought of practicalities, not emotions. However, I knew my promise was an empty one. Even if Joe's killer was found, I knew he or she wouldn't be brought to justice through the normal channels. This was a secret affair, and it was going to stay that way.

However, there might be something…

I thought about the animal smuggling ring. Last night had been a setup, but was that more proof that something was definitely going on and that someone was desperate to cover up the truth? Desperate enough to kill?

"If you crack it open, the press will love you," I said in a fairly bad imitation of my short-term publicity agent. I shivered a little as I remembered Colin. I was glad I'd persuaded my publishers, LightStrike, to never make an appointment like that again.

I turned and walked back towards the pet zone with redemption on my mind.

My phone rang again before I'd gone two paces. My, was I popular today!

"Hi Madi, it's Connie. I'm just calling to let you know that things are going great here. Business was already looking good, like you said it would, but since Halloween has come closer, everyone's piling in here chatting about murder." I could hear a dry amusement in her voice and was glad that my head chef saw the funny side. "You know… the balance sheet is looking pretty good. I think you should pop in and see it soon." There was a twinkle in her tone now that made me wonder… had I done it? Had I won my wager against Auryn?

"Thanks, Connie! I'll be sure to come in, well… tonight! It's the first cult… I mean… club meeting."

"How could I forget that it's tonight with everything that's been going on?! I'll see you then. Avery Zoo is doing well, by the way. As is The Lucky Zoo, or so I hear on the grapevine. Everyone's surprised the police aren't hanging around snooping this time, but I think it's for the best. All of the Halloween events are bringing in the punters."

For a second I frowned, wondering why Connie was the one imparting all of this news. Then I remembered that Tiff hadn't spoken to me since she'd warned me off any further research into her husband's past. It was all too clear from the unspoken apology in Connie's voice that she'd been asked to update me.

"I'm glad," I said, trying to sound pleased. Auryn and I had left our zoos in the hands of a hastily put together board. Usually, we didn't have anything resembling a board of directors. Instead, everyone was allowed a say. It meant that meetings often ran long, or even took an entire day, but it had made our zoos happy workplaces where everyone felt that they had a chance to make a difference. It was something I thought was severely lacking in every other zoo I'd visited.

"I almost forgot. Your lynx, Liberty, is really bringing in the crowds. I don't know if it's a macabre Halloween thing, but apparently visitors are enthralled by the fact that the lynx might have murdered someone... or helped them to do it." She tutted.

"People are weird," I said, echoing her sentiments. I silently despaired that what appealed to people was defi-nitely not what we tried to promote. I wanted to share sustainable zoo-life and a respect for all living creatures, great and small, with visitors to the zoo. They wanted murderous lynxes and cult-leader hangouts.

When I wished Connie goodbye and good luck with the rising tide of restaurant goers, I thought of Joe. Some little voice inside my head whispered that he'd have seen the funny side.

I arrived at the first meeting of the Ladies of the Common with a feeling of trepidation. I wasn't usually a nervous person, but the thought of having to wade through three metres deep of press who were out for my blood was one that made me itchy with nerves. However, when I'd parked up and walked towards The Wild Spot, I realised there wasn't a camera in sight. No one had sold us out.

I'd already known that it had been Nigel Wickington who was to blame for the press believing I was starting a cult, but it lifted my heart to know that all of the women Georgina and I had contacted were loyal.

I waved when I saw my lawyer friend standing outside of the restaurant waiting for me.

"Excited?" she asked with a big grin when she saw the nerves on my face.

"I am," I answered, realising it was true. I'd hated the Lords of the Downs ever since I'd learned of the club, and now I thought we might be on the path to cutting them down to size.

"I'm excited for the free food you promised us all."

"Hmmm… I don't remember that." I shot a pretend severe look at the lawyer, knowing she could persuade her way out of a high-security prison if she had to. "I have laid on some snacks and drinks though," I confessed. I'd wanted it to be a surprise for the women who turned up. It wasn't that I thought so dimly of the women we'd invited that I believed some would be motivated to attend by the thought of free food… but I knew if it were me, I sure as heck would be!

"You're so sweet," Georgina said, looking at me in a funny way for a second.

"Shall we?" I said, gesturing to the door when the moment went on for a few seconds too long.

Before I could open it, Connie rushed out, all smiles. "This is going to be great! I've put the food out and made a little plate up for you to have now, Madi, so no one thinks you're greedy later when the others arrive." She winked at me, her coffee complexion glowing with pleasure.

"Ahem! Thanks Connie," I said, doing my best to not look at Georgina.

We went inside and made small talk until the first club members arrived. All of them walked in wide-eyed, as if they, too, had been expecting the press to be out in force. I was pleased to inform them that no one had leaked our meeting's location or date.

It wasn't long before all of the tables were filled and I found myself standing up, looking around at a room full of local businesswomen who were fed up with being under the thumb. I smiled at several familiar faces, and the ladies nodded back at me.

It was time to begin the first ever meeting of the Ladies of the Common Club - or simply, 'The Common Sense Club' as one of the members had already told me she'd assumed we'd implied with our name.

One hour and a half later, we had the makings of our plan of action. Everyone had agreed we didn't want to be malicious. Fighting fire with fire just meant that everyone got burned. Instead, we would chip away at the Lords of the Downs' influence by making a parody of them. It was Poppy, head of Avery Zoo's reception team, who had come up with our campaign slogan 'Support local business women... and their men'. I'd been wary of Poppy ever since she'd replaced the late Jenna Leary, and I'd witnessed her flirting with my husband. It was only now that I realised I'd never given her a proper chance. She clearly knew more about the way things were in our local area than I'd given her credit for. It was the perfect slogan and summed up the way the Lords of the Downs were guilty of treating their female partners.

The other big decision we'd made was to hold a Halloween fete. A lot of the women worked in creative industries, and even those who didn't had pitched in, saying they wanted a chance to show off their business to other like-minded women and the local community - without needing to be worried about the Lords of the Downs frowning on an attention-seeking faux pas. With the local councillor who was in charge of taking bookings for the town square a club member, it was arranged and agreed right there and then. A Facebook event was made and everyone emailed out a newsletter that one of the ladies managed to throw together in what seemed like a matter of seconds.

"That's two hundred attendees already! Go Ladies of the Common!" Esme, an estate agent, called out just as I was wishing everyone a good night and thanking them all for coming. This news was met with a rapturous round of applause.

"Don't forget to submit your stall applications to me so I know how many tables to organise," Trinny, the councillor, reminded everyone as they gathered their bags and belongings and prepared to leave.

"I think we're a hit," Georgina said when the restaurant had cleared and we were left with the remnants of a good time had by all. "Did you see Annemarie Wickington's face? She looked like the cat who got the cream! She's had to put up with that rotten boys' club for years. Now it's all going to change."

"You really think so?" I asked.

Georgina nodded. "They can't touch us now that we're united. It's the perfect solution. It has been all along. All we needed was someone like you to bring it all together."

"And you," I added, knowing I was blushing.

Georgina shrugged like it was no big deal. I couldn't help but notice she'd become distracted from our conversation and was looking over to where Connie was tidying up the plates with another waitress who'd stayed on for the evening.

I looked back and forth between them and then back and forth again to check if I was reading things right.

"Georgina…" I began, unsure how to broach the subject.

The lawyer simply waved a hand at me and smiled. "Harry was enough to make anyone switch sides."

I smiled politely, knowing that she was surely kidding about that being the reason. But all the same, it was plain as day to me that Georgina was a big fan of Connie Breeze. I wondered if Connie would feel the same, and then realised it was none of my business.

"I need to be getting back. Comic work to do," I told the lawyer, slipping out of my seat and then nodding towards Connie.

Georgina watched me go with a twinkle in her eye. I left her to figure things out with Connie.

Tonight had been full of surprises.

9

BIGGER FISH

I approached my undercover mission at Corbyn Zoo with fresh zeal now that I'd nearly been shot. After much deliberation, Auryn and I had decided it did suggest that there was indeed an animal smuggling operation going on... and that we had to be close to finding the truth. It was frustrating knowing that the answer had to be right under our noses, hidden from us in some way. We redoubled our efforts, and even our reports to the zoo took shape in a such a way that made me think Corbyn Zoo would be pleased with what we'd picked up.

The truth, however, remained elusive until three days after my excursion with Lowell.

I was transporting a batch of ducklings from their heat-lamp quarters into the pet zone when I noticed it. In the corner of the large incubation room was an old unused metal pen with 'The Pet Zone' written on the attached plaque. It was the kind of pen where a sickly foal, kid, lamb, or calf might be kept under observation, but I knew from chatting to Robyn extensively that the pet zone's larger equine and cloven hoofed animals were all too elderly for birthing young these days. The goats and sheep seldom had problems either and when they did, Robyn had guiltily confessed she tended to take the ones that needed a bit of help home with her. Zoo protocol was to check on them every few hours and to just leave them to fend for themselves as much as possible but she couldn't bring herself to leave their survival down to chance. I'd written some strong words to management about their policy on that and hoped that it would soon change. If an animal could be saved, then why not save it? Animals always surprised you, no matter how bumpy their start in life. I believed they all needed a chance.

That was why I noticed the pen. For the most part, the metal was dull and covered in dust, showing its lack of use. However, the sign looked new, like it had recently been allocated to a zoo department that didn't need it. Plus, the top of the swing door into the pen was shiny... as if someone had been walking in and out. I walked over and ran a finger along the top. Definitely dust free. Then I looked at the pen itself. The floor was bare and there was absolutely nothing of interest inside. For a moment, I paused, lost in thought, before I followed my instincts and walked into the animal pen. Feeling faintly ridiculous, I tapped on the back wall.

It was hollow. What had looked like a wall was actually a panel of plasterboard that had been painted and moulded to blend with the rest of the stone wall. It had been done so well that you couldn't even see the outline of it. I pressed on it, hard, and the fake wall swung open.

"Just like Scooby Doo," I muttered before stepping into the darkness beyond the wall.

It took a while for my eyes to adjust to the gloom. I could hear things moving around in the dark and I quelled my natural urge to jump when my eyes played tricks on me. Instead, I took a deep breath and took out my phone, turning on the torch.

Creatures moved in the darkness and shining eyes glittered at me, reflecting the light from my phone. I drew in a breath and held it.

Joe was right.

He'd been right all along.

The smuggling operation was real... and it was happening at Corbyn Manor's Zoo Experience.

I walked past rows of tanks, noting that most of the animals in this dark room were reptilian or amphibian. Robyn's comment about the ease of smuggling eggs and smaller animals out of zoos had not been incorrect. However, there were some more unexpected additions. A cage filled with tiny hummingbirds all fluttering around their sugary food sources hung on the wall. Next to it, two young macaques looked back at me with doleful eyes as they clung to one another. For a moment, I tried to think of a logical explanation for why this eclectic bunch of animals would be crammed into a dark room together, but I could find no answer. That left only the truth - I'd stumbled upon the holding cells of animals ready for transport.

I was still peering into tanks and cages, trying to work out exactly which animals were here and who might be to blame, when I heard voices approaching. Then - horror of horrors - the swing gate of the enclosure creaked as it opened. I was seconds away from being discovered.

Animal eyes followed mine as I looked around desperately for a hiding place. A stack of cardboard boxes had been piled in the corner - perhaps used for packing some of the animals. I jumped into one without hesitation and then hunkered down, praying that no one would look inside.

I turned the light off on my phone the instant before the wall opened and light streamed in.

"How soon until the collection is made?" a female voice asked. I knew that I recognised it, but it took me a few moments to place. It was Jennifer Bucket. I sucked air silently in through my teeth. I'd imagined that the keepers themselves were running the illicit trade, fudging the numbers and keeping it quiet from their oblivious superiors. This was far worse. It went all the way to the top.

"Whenever they feel like it," a second voice drawled in response. "If they take too much longer, this lot will be past their sell-by date. And we are not taking a pay cut."

I frowned when I heard the male voice. He sounded familiar, too, but I couldn't place him. If only I could take a peek…

"Darren sounded nervous when I last spoke to him. I think he thinks someone is after us."

"Darren is always jumping at shadows. You'd think there were spies everywhere the way he talks." The man sounded amused.

I felt a bead of sweat slide down my back. If only he knew!

Their conversation diverted into discussing the health of various animals. As they moved around the room I opened my eyes, realising I'd clamped them shut, like a child who thinks hiding in their own darkness will conceal them. It was with some surprise that I realised I wasn't in total darkness. I'd shut the lid of the box when I'd squeezed myself in, but a narrow pin-prick of light was filtering through like a golden arrow. The smugglers must have found the light switch.

With silent promises to try harder at yoga, I bent forwards and tried to see out of the hole in the box.

I couldn't see much. It was at a bad angle, and all I was greeted by was the sight of two pairs of feet. One was clad in low kitten heels, as befitted a stylish, but practical, zoo manager. The other was a pair of dark green trainers that I happened to know formed part of a uniform. It was the jumpstart I needed to connect the dots and fill in the identity of the man in the room.

The animal smuggler was none other than Taylor Morningstar, the animal welfare officer who'd saved the lynx and inspected The Lucky Zoo.

I almost had to stop myself from bursting out of my hiding place and confronting them both. How could two people so involved in the care of animals be such traitors to their wellbeing? The fact that Taylor was actually an animal welfare officer was even more sickening. I balled and un-balled my fists whilst I restrained my urge to explode out of the box like a bat out of hell. The purpose of all of this was to gather evidence, not take down a small part of a huge operation. It was that thought and that thought alone that kept me in my hiding place.

Instead, I listened to their conversation patter on, and I considered why Taylor had caught the lynx alive and then given it to my zoo. That didn't make much sense at all, did it? I tried to think about it logically. Even if they'd shot Liberty, there would have still been DNA tests to figure out where she'd come from, and the whisper of smuggling would have still reached the right ears. As for passing the lynx onto me, I was in two minds about that. My first thought was that it had been a test to see if I would later be amenable to being approached by Taylor and signing my own private income deal. The second was that it had all been set up as a poetic preplanned method to dispatch anyone who went against them. I thought that my mind was getting a bit fanciful - probably due to the stuffy conditions in the box.

Joe had said he had a contact in the animal smuggling operation, but had they known they were being investigated, even then? I doubted it. Joe hadn't been a fool when it came to dealing with criminals. *Unless he trusted someone and they betrayed him,* I suddenly thought. There seemed to be a lot of that going round lately...

"Anyway, we should get packing boxes. You've made it so that it won't be missed from the food stores?" Taylor asked, causing my ears to prick up.

The sweat was sliding freely down my back now. I was surely only seconds away from being discovered!

"Of course," Jennifer batted back. "I run a tight ship here. No one is going to question anything I do."

Their footsteps approached, getting closer and closer with every passing instant. I racked my brains for any plausible excuse as to why I was squashed inside a cardboard box, eaves-dropping on their secret conversation. I might be a creative thinker, but even my comic-writing brain drew a big fat blank.

I heard a hand brush the cardboard just above my head. I sucked in a breath, ready to burst out and try to rush them. Perhaps in the surprise I would be able to get out of the room and out into the relative safety of the zoo. What could they do to me then? The whole undercover operation would be blown, but at least I'd get out alive...

"What was that?" The hand was withdrawn from the top of the box.

"What?" Taylor said, but then fell silent.

In the quiet, I realised I could hear it, too. There was someone in the room outside.

"I told you we should have soundproofed the place!" Jennifer hissed.

"You told me that pretty much no one outside of the circle ever came in here, beyond that fluffy bunny pet keeper. Then you went and hired her a helper who's got her feet much more firmly planted."

"Madigan Amos? She's not supposed to be focusing on the animals. She's supposed to be reporting back on what our keepers are up to and who's screwing around and ripping us off."

"I told you from the start that was a bad idea. She notices things! But you didn't think that paying someone to snoop around might be a bad idea when we've got something to hide? That's probably her right now."

"I'll deal with it," Jennifer growled back. "I wasn't the one who okayed her employment. That was the rest of the board. I could hardly veto it on the grounds that she might figure out our little side game, could I?"

"She knows the history of that lynx who got loose. She could be onto us," Taylor said.

I'd been saying silent prayers to whoever it was that was walking around in the other room, but now I felt a stab of worry about my own safety in the future. I would have to watch my back and my front and... well - everything.

There was another silence that hinted the person in the other room had gone. My momentary relief was replaced once more with panic, as I realised that they were going to come back and carry on the work they'd been about to do.

A loud, blaring siren cut through the air, causing several of the animals to squeak in alarm. It was only now that I realised why the smugglers hadn't bothered to soundproof the room. Most of the animals in their care were simply too young to make much of a fuss.

"Is it a drill? What is it?" Taylor said, sounding exasperated.

"We don't have drills in this building, it worries the animals too much," Jennifer snapped back. "It's got to be real. That, or someone is messing around."

"What about the animals?"

"Leave them. It doesn't matter."

Once more, I felt like I'd been punched in the stomach by

this woman's lack of regard for the animals she was supposed to be in charge of overseeing the care for.

I waited for them to be well and truly gone before I rocked the box over and was spilled out onto the floor. I'd been so tightly packed in I'd found that there wasn't any other way to get out of my situation.

The darkness was penetrated once more when the wall opened and light streamed in. My heart jumped into my mouth, as I feared one of the bad guys had come back for something - perhaps some animal worth enough money that it did warrant the effort of saving.

"This just got interesting, didn't it?" Lowell said, standing with his hands on his hips and looking around at all of the cages. "A secret smuggling room. It's not original, but somehow it seems to have been working for them this far."

"How did you know I was in here?"

Lowell brushed a hand back through his dark hair. "Now, don't get angry… but you know I've been watching you for Katya. I still am. Anyway, you know how to get into trouble like no one else I've ever met."

"I suppose I should be thanking Katya then," I said, unwilling to accept that Lowell had done it out of any other reason. He was just doing his job.

"Madi, I set that alarm off because I care about you. Katya said I should keep an eye on you, not rescue you from perilous situations. I could have just sat back and watched.

"How noble of you to make the effort to press an alarm."

Lowell sighed and shrugged his shoulders. "Think what you want. I do still care about you. You have no idea how much I wish things happened differently between us. I know it's too late now, but that doesn't mean I'm ready to let it go."

I looked up into his serious dark eyes. I knew mine were clouded by distrust and past experience, but I tried to put it aside and look again. This time, I thought he might be telling the truth.

"We should go. They'll realise it was a false alarm soon and they'll be suspicious," I said, deciding that practical matters were more important now than unresolved emotional ties.

Lowell inclined his head and said nothing more. We exited the building the back way and walked silently back to the MI5 shed.

"Do you know who the man was?" Lowell asked once we were inside.

"Yes. And he knows who I am." I quickly explained how I'd met Taylor and what he already knew of me and my involvement with potentially smuggled animals. "It's not going to take much for him to put two and two together and figure out why I'm really here. Heck, he'll probably call the entire thing off and disappear."

"I don't think so," Lowell said, surprising me. "These guys aren't in the same league as the money launderers we've hunted for years. You saw all of those animals in the back there. They'll have to make one last shipment before going to ground. Otherwise, they'll lose their stock and their pay check. After all of the number fiddling they've done, they can hardly pop them back where they belong, can they?"

I shrugged. They'd managed to sneak them out once already, and I had a strong feeling that Jennifer wasn't the only one making money on the side at Corbyn Manor. I would definitely be looking very closely at the primate department, the couple in charge of the birds, and the reptile and amphibian keepers.

"I think it's time we bring others in. We're running out of time. If we don't act now, this whole thing could slip through our fingers," Lowell announced.

I shook my head fervently. "This is just supposed to be an

evidence gathering mission! We can't blow everything. It might all be over anyway. Taylor will know that looking round zoos and fixing them up is what I do. After Joe's death, it's also common knowledge that I've been threatened. It's therefore logical that I would have some protection around me."

"You're clutching at straws. We should strike!" Lowell protested.

"We'll take out a tiny portion of the operation. From what Joe said, this barely scrapes the surface. I want the smuggling gone - eradicated. I don't want to pat myself on the back for catching a few crooks."

Lowell gnashed his teeth for a moment, before relenting. "Fine. I supposed all we risk is letting a few minnows slip the net. If they think they've got away, they might be more stupid the next time."

I nodded enthusiastically before foolishly adding: "Anyway, we don't know who we can trust."

Lowell looked sharply at me. "There is no traitor in MI5. We were infiltrated, somehow… but it wasn't a person. It couldn't have been. We were all checked - everyone in the operation."

I shrugged and let it go. It wasn't my battle to fight. "You're in contact with Katya, aren't you? Can you please do me one huge favour…" I looked him full in the face, hoping to turn on the charm. His frown said I was probably hugely messing it up, but I was willing to keep trying for my old friend. "Can you please tell her that I'm sorry for hiding the truth from her? I know it was just as bad as…" I trailed off, remembering who I was talking to. "And also tell her I forgive her for asking you to spy on me."

"That was to help you!"

I waved a hand. "I'm willing to overlook it."

"We're getting nowhere with this case, by the way,"

Lowell said, gesturing to the still of Joe's last video on screen. It didn't escape my notice that he hadn't agreed or disagreed to my request. I supposed I'd just have to wait and see.

"Leona told me pretty much nothing. It's strange, but I definitely got the impression that she was out of the loop. Maybe the launderers are scattered, and this is nothing to do with them." I was clutching at straws. There were so many maybes I could fill a book. "At least no one's tried to kill me. Well, apart from in the park… but that was different."

"Yeah, I know," Lowell said, not sounding nearly as thrilled as I was at the prospect of no one trying to murder me. "I think we're going to have to pull out of here soon and hand it all back over to the local police."

"You haven't found anything?" I said, bemused by the amount of manpower that had been dedicated to this case and the lack of tangible results. It also sounded like they were just going to leave me to fend for myself. What if that was exactly what the murderer was waiting for?

"We don't even know why Joe died," I said, feeling saddened by the prospect of justice not being served. Joe had possessed his fair share of faults, but the more I looked into his death, the more I was convinced that he'd genuinely changed sides before the end. I wasn't sure his motivation was something I exactly approved of, but I was grateful for his help all the same.

"It's probably something petty. We were wrong to think he was important," Ms Borel announced striding into the shed with Flannigan dogging her heels. "We thought that either the people responsible were his old colleagues he tried to run from, or that one of their enemies got to him first."

Flannigan let out a squeaky 'tsk-tsk' of amusement. "Probably just got himself shafted by one of these angry PR people you told us about. It's amazing how something so small and inconsequential can mean the world to somebody.

Humans are willing to kill for so little." Flannigan shook his head as if imparting some great piece of philosophy.

I found myself rising to the bait. "How would they have known to dump him in the lynx enclosure? Why would they have conveniently left that contract in his pocket - the contract that was supposed to make me look bad?! What about the the deliberate disfiguration? That wasn't all down to Liberty. Someone wanted him to need to have an ID. It's the same person who's playing us all for fools, who nearly got Lowell and me killed." I bit my tongue and blushed in embarrassment when I realised I'd used the wrong name for my ex-boyfriend. The bottom line was, Lowell was how I'd known him and how I would always know him.

"He could have been carrying that document on him to use as some kind of leverage against you. Disfigurement is a common sign of a passionate crime. Perhaps this PR competitor thought he'd disfigured their success and decided to return the favour."

"The document was out of date, and Joe would have known it," I countered. I was certain it had been dredged up by someone to put the cat amongst the pigeons. "What about the lynx being chosen? What about the killer knowing where the ladder was kept?"

"This will have been a long-term buildup of emotion. They'll probably have watched Joe over a period of time. That's plenty of opportunity for them to learn where supplies are kept. They might have picked the lynx enclosure because it's pretty popular, right?"

I nodded. That much was true.

"But what about the gunmen in the park..." I wasn't going to let them write this whole thing off as being the work of some lone madman. This was a conspiracy!

"We don't actually know they were there for us. You said

Leona split pretty fast. She's got enemies, too," Lowell pointed out, ever so reasonably.

I stared at him. I couldn't believe he was siding with his bosses in this!

"We've got a new lead in the laundering case up in Liverpool. We'll wrap things up and be gone in a couple of days. Of course, it goes without saying that this is all covered within the act you signed," Flannigan said, boringly as ever.

I made sure I didn't look at Lowell when I nodded meekly in agreement. He was no doubt still exceedingly annoyed that I'd told Auryn what he'd guessed I had.

"I'm sure you'll be grateful for some normalcy," Ms Borel said with what I believed passed for a smile.

"It will be nice to have things go back to normal," I confessed, realising that I wasn't going to get anywhere by protesting. I would just have to let them go.

And then it would be down to me.

10

FOOLS RUSH IN

As promised, a day later the case was handed back to the Gigglesfield police force. Detective Gregory wasted no time hauling me back in for an interview, and I was raked over the coals again with regard to Joe's video, my knowledge that he was a wanted criminal, and (I strongly suspected) for sticking my nose into the detective's business. Beating the truth out of suspects may no longer be acceptable, but I felt like I'd taken a battering all the same when Detective Gregory started to wrap things up.

"You know why I was trying to find out about your past, don't you?" I asked, feeling like a used punchbag.

"You couldn't let your friend be happy. You had to insert some drama." This was the flippant manner in which I'd been questioned during the interview.

"Of course not. It's because I love her. Just like I hope you love her."

"Of course I do. She's the best thing to ever happen to me."

For a moment we were caught in deadlock, both eyeing the other, trying to figure out what was coming next.

"Then why keep the truth from her? It always comes out in the end," I said, trying to impart some hard-learned wisdom. Even if he hated me, he should do that much for Tiff and their unborn child.

"We're honest with each other." He still thought he could keep his cards close to his chest.

"I know you worked with MI5…"

"…Who hasn't? I work for the police. We work with the security service."

"…and you've worked for the other side, too."

Now Detective Gregory hesitated. "The other side?" A smirk was already on his face.

"I don't know what group of people it was, or what they were guilty of, but it was enough to get you in trouble with *them*, wasn't it? That's why you were held to ransom, doing *their* dirty work as a mercenary. You thought you were coming to Gigglesfield for some peace and quiet, but someone tricked you…" I'd decided I believed Lowell's story. It was exactly the sort of thing Lowell would do without thinking through the consequences. Some things would never change.

"You don't know anything," the detective said, turning red.

"That's right. I don't. And I don't want to know any details. If you want to share them with Tiff or not, that's your decision, but I think you should share something. It's not fair on her otherwise. What if the next time one of your old enemies breaks into your house you're not there to stop them before they get to her?"

Detective Gregory ground his teeth together. "It was a one off. This town is supposed to be easy to forget about. I'm supposed to be forgotten. That was just bad luck."

I raised my eyebrows at him, imploring him to think seriously about what he was saying.

It took a while, but in the end, his shoulders relaxed. "I'll tell her. Not everything. No one would want to know that." His face was grave when he said it, and I found that I believed he meant it for Tiff's own good. "But, I will tell her my past and who I've worked for. Better I do it myself." He raised his eyes when he said it. I saw the question written there.

"She'll be angry - mostly with herself for not suspecting - but I think she'll forgive you. That's what love is all about, right?" I said, before remembering everything that had happened between Lowell and me, and how it hadn't exactly held true for us.

"We shouldn't be enemies," the detective said making it sound like some colossal effort.

"We shouldn't," I agreed. "We both care for Tiff, and we need to be on the same side." I bit my lip for a moment, remembering that I wasn't even sure if Tiff still wanted to be my friend after our last discussion. Even Alex coming clean might not wipe the slate clean. I would never gloat about being right, but her own annoyance with herself for not seeing it could easily transfer onto me.

"I don't know if you know, but the club I'm a part of is holding a Halloween fete for businesses…"

"I know about it all right," Detective Gregory cut in. "I've had the mayor chewing my ear off trying to get me to cancel it on the grounds that it breaches the peace."

My mouth dropped open. "The mayor?!"

"Wesley Jones." I recognised the name from the Lords of the Downs. No surprises there. "Before you complain, I refused. The proper planning is in place - albeit at short notice. There is nothing to stop you having your fete."

Unless I was much mistaken, the ghost of a smile crossed the detective's face, but it was gone before I could blink. It didn't surprise me to learn that Detective Gregory wasn't the exclusive club's biggest fan. They'd invited him to their business awards evening as the honorary law enforcement guest, but I'm sure he suspected, as I did, that they'd known from the start that the detective had been due to be dragged in for questioning in a murder investigation. They'd wanted a little drama to spice up the evening's entertainment, and Alex Gregory was not a man who forgave easily.

"Well... good," I said, rather flustered by the lengths the Lords of the Downs were going to stop us in our tracks. "I wanted Tiff to be a member of the club, but I know why she didn't come to the first meeting. Could you maybe tell her that there's a stall for her at the fete if she wants it? I would love her to be there."

"I'll do that for you... right after I've told her about my past. If she's still talking to either of us at the end of it, I'm sure she'll be thrilled."

I beamed at the detective. "That's brilliant! How's the case coming on?"

Detective Gregory's expression closed down. "I'm not at liberty to discuss any of the details."

"So much for being friends," I said, not being serious.

The detective sighed as if the day had been a very long one. It was only ten in the morning. I tried not to be offended.

When I was free from the confines of the station, I thought about what had changed to make me remove my suspicion from Detective Gregory. I supposed there was nothing beyond my feeling that he was trying to be an honest man and do what was best for the woman he loved. It was that which made me sure he hadn't been the one to kill Joe Harvey. He would never have brought that kind of trouble home with him in such a deliberate way, when he was clearly trying so hard to keep it from his door.

There was one plus from the investigation being handed

over to the local police force. They didn't have the staff to investigate every bit of post that came my way and spend hours mulling over what Joe's mysterious video really meant. That was why I'd been given a copy on DVD and told to call them if I had any blinding flashes of inspiration. There may have been some sarcasm involved when Detective Gregory had said that last part, but I'd chosen to ignore it in the interests of our hopefully blossoming relationship.

I wasn't sure why I watched the video again that night. Perhaps I was just as desperate as MI5 had been, or perhaps I was starting to miss what Joe had brought to my life. Either way, I watched the darn thing several times before something finally clicked.

It was right before Joe did his little dramatic turn, stroking the plant wall behind him and brushing his hair back 'a-la Hollywood'. He warned that a person who'd turned their cloak once would turn it again easily. I'd known when I'd first watched the video that he'd been heavily hinting that there was a double agent on one side or the other - something that MI5 had decided to brush away (at least - as far as infiltration of their own ranks went) but now it was really making me think. Something that Flannigan had said came back to me. *Humans are willing to kill for so little.* Now that I thought about it, I wondered if he'd imparted more than he knew. Joe's death had been set up to look like many things it wasn't, but what if the truth was much simpler? Joe had known who it was that was working with MI5 and with his laundering gang, and when he'd gone missing, the turncoat had assumed the worst and killed him. Had Flannigan been that man?

I furiously racked my brains, trying to figure out if he'd

given anything away beyond a vague statement implying that not a lot was needed to lead to murder. There'd been the time I'd caught him in the records room. I'd definitely got the impression that he hadn't wanted to be discovered. Had I considered what he was really doing there? Was it that plausible that he'd been forced to go through zoo records because of a lack of permission from the zoo? I knew the way MI5 worked, and I found it surprising that they would be so considerate of something like privacy. They'd certainly invaded mine enough times without a care in the world!

But what else could he have been looking for?

It was something I needed to check.

I bit my lip. What else was bothering me? I thought back again and remembered... Flannigan had known about the animal smuggling happening at the zoo before I'd told him. Looking back, I'd completely missed it... but now it all felt like it was coming together.

"I've got to do something. He's behind it all," I muttered, feeling a mixture of dread and elation. It swirled around in my stomach and made me feel quite sick.

Acting on impulse I pulled my phone out and dialled Katya's number. The voice on the end of the line informed me that the person I was trying to contact was not available at the moment. I considered leaving a message, but some instinct inside me whispered that Katya would have answered if she'd wanted to hear from me.

With a sigh, I gave up. For a moment I hesitated before going online and taking down Lowell's number from his phoney private detective page. I'd deleted his contact details long ago, as every time I saw his name it made me mad.

When Lowell answered the phone without a question in his voice, I deduced that he hadn't done the same for me.

"Katya's not answering my calls," I explained before realising that, if I wanted Lowell to pass along a message, I'd have to tell him my theories. And there was no way he was going to believe it.

"What am I telling her?" Lowell asked with the tone of a bored teenager forced to pass notes between two frenemies.

"Just that I have important news I need to share with her. Urgently."

"Uh-huh. What would that news be?"

I bit my lip. "Is this line safe?"

"We're not in a film. It's fine. No one's listening."

"Okay… I think Flannigan is the double agent," I said and gave him the brief version of why.

Lowell was silent for a while when I'd finished. "Have you considered the possibility that this is all some final joke of the man you knew as Joe Harvey? I'm not saying he caused his own death, but it might have amused him to toy with those who looked into it - should the eventuality ever arrive. He had enemies working for the company. It would be just like him to try to throw suspicion on an old enemy."

"I'm not naive!" I crossly informed my ex-boyfriend. "Joe didn't fake Flannigan snooping around in an office room claiming he was going over employee records, and Joe didn't tell Flannigan about the animal smuggling ring he mysteriously had prior knowledge of." I hesitated. "Or perhaps he did… and that's the whole point. He knew! He's the double agent!"

"MI5 has a lot of fingers in a lot of pies. If something is going on in this country, you can believe they know all about it. I know the animal smuggling is very important to you but when it's measured against national security concerns, things like that often receive less workforce dedication."

"You mean they get to carry on unstopped," I said, unamused.

"Yes." Lowell confessed. "But it's entirely plausible that

Flannigan already knew about the smuggling problem because it's his business to know."

I ground my teeth, frustrated by Lowell and how reasonable he was being.

"I'll find out what he was looking for in that room," I promised and hung up, just as annoyed as I'd suspected I'd end up if I called Lowell. We may not be together, or even particularly friendly, but he still knew how to press all of my buttons. It annoyed the heck out of me.

For a moment I allowed myself to wallow in self-pity. I'd managed to alienate two of my best friends during the past two weeks and things weren't looking up. All I could console myself with was that I was getting closer to the truth everyday... and then those guilty would be made to pay.

———

Then it happened, and everything changed.

Auryn told me that one of his team members had turned their back on a child. The child had promptly vanished inspiring mass panic. Whilst the others had run around the zoo, Auryn had headed for the staff-only areas. He'd claimed that he'd tried to get into the mindset of the kid, and had known that he personally would have headed for the very place he was forbidden to go. I had another idea that Auryn had wanted to escape the mayhem for a quiet five minutes.

He'd been poking around behind barns and old exhibits that had been left to rust when he'd found the child. The boy was playing in the dirt, poking at an ants' nest with a stick. Auryn had been on the verge of seizing him and hauling him back to the entertainment team, when he'd heard voices and realised that they weren't alone. He'd explained that he could only assume he'd subconsciously recognised the voices, because he'd slid down behind a large empty barrel and waited.

"It's Tuesday. I gave them our final offer and they agreed. I should probably be thanking you for employing someone to snoop around… nothing like the fear of being discovered to make slow clients move faster," a male voice had said.

"She doesn't know anything. She's far too focused on the assignment we've given her." I'd been secretly smug when Auryn had imparted what Jennifer had said. Never underestimate the focus of a workaholic when it came to working on multiple animal-related assignments at once!

"You'd better be right. Otherwise, I'll have to clean up your mess." Taylor had replied. Auryn had emphasised that he hadn't meant it in a cheery way.

"Pick up is at eleven fifteen. Be ready to pack and ship," he'd finished, before Auryn had heard footsteps walking away. It was only then that he'd realised the other man had been on the other side of the fence.

In true child style, the ant poker had picked that moment to scream at the tiny civilisation he was attacking. Auryn had pressed himself against the barrel and prayed that neither party would look round and see him when Jennifer had shouted out 'Who's there?'. She must have then discovered who her eavesdropper was because the next time he'd heard her voice she'd sounded much less ferocious. Auryn had waited until she'd led her charge away before he'd crawled out of his hiding place.

Whether or not he'd returned to work immediately or had 'looked' for the child a little longer, I wasn't sure.

After the initial excitement of knowing that something was happening, Auryn and I convened in the woods beyond the zoo at lunchtime. We'd discovered that no one tended to venture beyond the zoo's walls. So, unlike Taylor and Jennifer, we weren't overheard.

"We can't do this on our own. It's too dangerous. We have no idea what we're up against," Auryn said once we'd discussed everything he'd overheard.

"I would have asked Katya," I said, feeling gloomy all over again. Then my mind cleared for a moment. "Detective Gregory. We could ask him!"

Auryn looked at me like I'd gone completely crazy.

"We're trying to build bridges... for Tiff's sake! Anyway, it would be good to have the police on our side. I bet the detective would bring a few trusted members of the police force with him, too."

Auryn eyed me speculatively. "What happened to thinking he was the double agent?"

I waved a hand. "I've already explained all of that to you. I don't believe Alex Gregory is the bad guy here. He genuinely does want to settle down in a quiet town and try to forget his past. He's not faking it." For the briefest of moments, I thought back to my own relationship where the other party had been lying to me. Did I think Lowell had been faking everything, now that I knew the entire truth? I didn't think so. It was all ancient history now, but I realised I did believe he'd had feelings for me at one point. He'd just made the wrong choice.

"What about Lowell?" Auryn said, as if reading my mind.

I nodded reluctantly. "Just so long as we can convince him not to tell his boss."

"You really think Flannigan is the one working for the other side? I thought you suspected Lowell, too?"

I bit my lip for a second, chewing it over. "I'm still not sure," I confessed. Lowell was, unfortunately, still a candidate. He'd come into contact with smugglers before, he was definitely adept at lying, and I only had his word that Katya had confided so much in him, as we were out of contact with one another. "But what choice do we have? If we have him with us, at least we'll know exactly where he is."

After it was agreed, I made the call to both Lowell and the detective. After a brief three-way discussion everything was arranged and a plan was formulated.

"Remember - this isn't a sting, it's a reconnaissance mission," Lowell had reminded me several times during our conversation.

"This isn't an excuse to go rushing in. We're gathering evidence only!" Detective Gregory had contributed when I called him.

I'd ended both conversations feeling miffed. Did people really think I blindly rushed into situations without thinking about the potential consequences?

I'd put the question to Auryn.

He'd masterfully dodged it.

11

OLD FRIENDS, NEW BEGINNINGS

The Halloween fete was held three days before we were due to attempt our reconnaissance mission. Even though it was the final day of October, and there was a distinctly icy bite in the air, the weather held, and the preemptive tarpaulins weren't needed to shelter the many stall holders. Right before we were due to officially open, I looked around at everything before me and felt a huge sense of pride. Everyone had come through. The fete looked magnificent, and I just knew it was going to be a success!

"Spotted any spies yet?" Georgina asked, sliding up next to me. She handed me a t-shirt. I raised my eyebrows at the Ladies of the Common branded item of clothing. It looked great.

"Someone can work fast!" I commented.

Georgina snorted. "That's what happens when you don't have a committee of stuffy wealthy men to hold you back. No one feels restricted or worried by any repercussions. We're not playing around at being politicians."

I nodded in agreement. So far, the Ladies of the Common

was going great. However, everyone had been told to be on the look out for potential sabotage attempts. All of us had discussed at great length how petty it would be if the Lords of the Downs were to strike against us. I'd racked my brains over what they could possibly do to ruin things, but I privately thought they'd played all of their cards. The men who ran the club didn't actually get their hands dirty. They moved their chess pieces around the board and tried to psyche people out and manipulate them into doing what they wanted. They didn't turn up with pitchforks.

I put my t-shirt on and walked through the fete. When I turned the first corner, I saw a flash of strawberry blonde as a woman placed a large bag on an empty stall, before hurriedly attempting to unpack it.

"Tiff!" I called out, immediately thrilled that my best friend had decided to accept my invitation to have a stall at the Halloween fete.

She turned to face me with a tentative smile on her face. "How are you? I'm sorry I'm late. I didn't feel too well." She ran a hand across her belly when she said it.

"That's no problem at all! We're only just about to open. I hope you're feeling better now? And I'm fine. I'm doing great." Well, I was now anyway!

"Me too," Tiff replied, smiling back a lot more openly. "Alex told me everything by the way," she said as I helped her to unpack her maps.

I waited to find out what 'everything' meant. I wasn't about to put my big fat foot in it again.

"He told me about who he used to work for - once I'd figured it out and told him that I was clued in." Tiff shot me a curiously sympathetic look, that I thought probably meant Alex now thought I was just as crazy as Lowell did for opening my mouth and filling in my friends. "He also said about the mistakes he'd made and how he'd wanted to change all that when he came to town. Even though he was basically tricked into coming here, he says he's the happiest he's ever been and knows that this place and me are his home." She was practically glowing when she said it. "Our family is everything to him."

"Good, I'm so glad," I said, meaning it with every fibre.

"I'm sorry for biting your head off and avoiding you. You were right that Alex was hiding something, and I understand you were looking out for me. I also want to say thanks for bringing Alex in on the case you're working," Tiff said, lowering her voice for the last part. "I think you guys are going to be great friends in no time at all!"

I managed a weak smile in return. I wasn't so sure 'great friends' was on the cards, but perhaps tolerable acquaintances.

After a happy reunion, I admired Tiff's Halloween themed fantasy maps and then set off to look around the rest of the fete. I waved to Gloria when I walked down the last strip. I'd told her about the fete and explained that it wouldn't exactly sell more books but it would be good for community spirit. She'd surprised me by jumping at the idea. Today she was standing behind the stall ordering around a young-looking female intern. Some things never changed.

She waved to me and pointed at the mockup of my forth-coming comic book release. "Doesn't it look fantastic?"

I nodded enthusiastically, knowing it was what Gloria wanted. I'd approved the cover art the week before, but it was something else to see it in real life.

"Is everything going okay?" I asked, raising my eyebrows slightly. I'd been warned that the bad publicity I was receiving could damage my comic's success. Readers seeking wholesome comics might be put off by the press implying that I'd murdered a man and thrown him into the lynx enclosure.

Gloria sounded chipper about the whole thing. "Nothing to worry about! To tell you the truth, preorders have been through the roof. I don't know what to tell you - people love drama! Not that I condone murder - but a bit of notoriety never hurt anyone."

I nodded, thinking that it had held true so far. However, it certainly wasn't worth killing for.

Which I definitely hadn't done.

After telling her how thrilled I was, I ventured onwards to meet the other female stallholders. Even though I'd sensed what a wonderful community of local women we had when we'd convened for our first meeting, it was quite another thing to see it laid out in front of me in such a colourful display. I passed by bakery stalls, arts and crafts, and some far more unusual fare. All comers were welcome at the Halloween fete.

Well… nearly all. I did feel a pang of regret that we'd turned away male-represented businesses, even though they weren't necessarily in with the Lords of the Downs. It was unfair, but it was the line we had to take in order to properly combat the autocratic rule that had gripped Gigglesfield for too long.

I paused by a blade-smith and admired her knives and swords. She cheerily professed that she didn't really expect to sell any of the rather intimidating blades, but wasn't it wonderful to have the chance to inspire others to take up the trade?

I moved on to what I believed was a regular plant-seller, but she turned out to specialise in all kinds of herbs.

"They're so versatile! I swear I could tell you a million uses for basil that people just don't consider. It's more than just something to throw in with spaghetti. Did you know, it's been used as a spice and in medicine for at least 5000 years? There are also more than 160 different types of basil, which vary in both looks and flavour. I really like lemon basil and cinnamon basil - definitely more interesting than your supermarket variety." She said it like it was a dirty word.

"I didn't know any of that," I confessed, being blissfully ignorant when it came to plants. I'd once had a spider plant, but it had turned up its toes as soon as I'd settled it in on a windowsill. With hindsight, I wasn't so sure I hadn't confused the pot of water I'd been using to spritz it with and the window cleaner I'd kept next to it. The only plants I'd ever had survive were the ones in the garden that kept themselves to themselves. The living walls at the zoo were quite rightly entrusted to an experienced groundskeeper. However, after hearing Rachel talk, I was definitely toying with the idea of a herb garden.

"And this is sorrel. Look at the beautiful red veins that run through these leaves. Isn't it stunning? It's mostly cultivated as an ornamental plant these days. However, you can use it to make a great lemonade-type drink! It's also used in folk medicine to treat bruises. Isn't that fascinating?"

I admired the leafy green plant.

"You know... you've got a lot of herbs at your zoo. When I visited, I must confess I spent more time looking at your living walls and roofs than the animals." Rachel grinned.

I smiled back. "I forgive you. We all have our different interests."

We talked a little while longer, and she sold me on the herb garden idea. I ended up walking away from her stall with several tiny potted plants and the sneaking suspicion that they would all be dead within a week.

When the fete was well underway and I was lost in a whirl of pleasantries and congratulations on how things were going, I saw Detective Gregory walking towards me.

"Did someone call the police?" I asked, arching an eyebrow. It wouldn't surprise me if one of our rival club's members had called them in as some last ditch attempt at sabotage.

His lips curved up a little. "No... I'm here for Tiff and to see what some of the town's businesses have to offer. It's a great event." He inclined his head and looked at me seriously. I knew it was great praise indeed coming from a man who didn't always see eye to eye with me.

"How's the case coming on?"

The detective shot me a look that let me know I hadn't been subtle. It made it all the more surprising when he actually answered.

"Not well. I'm not sure if you're aware, but the body hasn't been released yet due to the nature of the case and the lack of relations to the deceased. We've gone over it with a fine tooth comb but there's nothing. It's completely clean from, well... everything, if you exclude anything that occurred post mortem. It has all the signs of a professional job. That, or..." He trailed off without finishing his sentence.

"What?" I pressed, knowing he was probably telling me more than he should, but desperately wanting him to continue. "Joe was my friend. I want to know your theory," I emphasised.

Detective Gregory looked around in such a dramatic way I half expected a spy to fall out of one of the giant flowerpots that surrounded the town square. "The people who investigated this case originally might have removed the evidence. I don't know why they would, but it is a possibility. You don't look surprised," the detective continued when I remained stoney-faced.

"I think there is something rotten at the core of their organisation and I think that rot could be spreading."

The detective looked at me like I'd sprouted horns. "If you say so. It was probably just a professional job."

I shrugged it off. I hardly had enough evidence to

convince myself of anything, let alone someone else. All the same, there was something niggling away in my brain… it whispered I was missing something. Why did brains do that to you?

"Look out," I heard one of the stallholders say.

I turned away from the detective to look down the aisle of stalls. Nigel Wickington was striding along towards me looking like he was on the war path.

"Thanks for coming, Nigel!" I said, greeting him with my sunniest smile. "It means a lot to have your support." Okay, so perhaps I was looking for a fight, too.

All around, I noticed the silence spreading. It was as if the entire world was holding their breath. I was ready to make my stand.

"I'm not here for that!" He bristled right back at me. "I just wanted to say, er…" He looked around at the watching eyes and did some more harrumphing. "I think it's time we engage in some sort of agreement." He made to motion me away from the crowded square, but I wasn't going to give him any leeway. After years of pushing local businesses around, I thought everyone deserved to hear what he had to say.

"Let's call a truce. All of this stuff is ridiculous."

"What stuff?" I asked, raising my eyebrows at him.

A red glow crept across the older man's face. "I just mean this is a demonstration. I see no reason why our two clubs can't co-exist." He looked over to the right where two rows of stalls away I could see Annemarie Wickington watching him with her hands on her hips. She nodded her head once in his direction and Nigel reluctantly continued. "Are you amenable to that idea?"

I thought about it. "Yes… but with one or two conditions attached."

Nigel seemed to deflate, but surely he had to have known it was coming.

"Whatever we do within our clubs is our business... however, clubs shall have no effect on which businesses are favoured over others. Also, we will work together to further the success of all of our local businesses. We owe the town that much. No more favours. No more autocracy." I looked at him with steel in my gaze.

The wind blew and leaves fell to the ground with a gentle sigh. I half expected tumbleweed to roll on by.

"Fine." he said after much inner teeth-gnashing.

I made to extend my hand for a shake, but he'd already turned and walked away. "I think that went well?" I muttered to myself before Annemarie Wickington arrived beside me.

"There, it's all sorted now," she said, proudly. I wondered just how much pressure she'd had to put on her husband in order to force him to make such a huge concession. "Now there'll be no more silliness around here."

"I hope you're right," I said, silently wishing for a quiet time in life. This past year and a bit had felt like something straight out of an action thriller.

The rest of the fete passed pleasantly with no further calls for drama. Everyone who was selling things sold a lot, and the rest were all very pleased with the amount of support there'd been and the number of people who hadn't previously had a clue that their little corner of Gigglesfield had existed. I was thrilled that everything had come together so well, and the clamour was already beginning for a similar event to be held before Christmas.

I was helping to pack up my publisher's stall when a male voice said my name. I turned around to discover Drew James standing there.

"It's good to see you," he said, smiling that charming smile of his. I'd known that he hadn't served prison time for the crimes he'd committed, but I was still surprised to see him strolling around in the centre of Gigglesfield when people he'd wronged were present.

"What can I do for you?" I asked, forced to show him more politeness than I had on the phone due to the presence of many listening ears. The last thing I wanted to do was set the tongues of the local gossips wagging.

"It's more what I can do for you," he said, dropping in a salacious wink.

I tried to walk away right there and then, but he reached out and grabbed my arm. I looked down at his hand and he released it with an apology.

"I have information you should know. It's about your zoo. Just let me say it, please."

I gave him a steady look - one that promised I would walk away for good if he tried to move the conversation onto anything else. I wouldn't have normally entertained a man like Drew, but I had a nasty feeling that until he'd said whatever he wanted to say, he wasn't going to leave me alone.

"Thank you." He beamed at me and then toned it down a few watts, remembering my warning. "When I watched the property deed being discussed with the Abraham family, back when I was a lowly tea-maker, I remember there being a strange condition. They bought the old farm and the land surrounding it, but there was something extra thrown in. The old farmer's brother lived in what was essentially a shack across the hills from where your zoo is. The land that the shack was built on and the surrounding area were technically part of the farm plot. They were included in the sale, on the condition that the land and property would belong to the brother until his death. I saw his obituary in the papers just last week." He raised his eyebrows at me.

"Are you saying that I own more land than I realise?"

He nodded. "There might be a few legal technicalities to

jump through, and you'll have to get a hold of that original deed of sale, but no one else has a claim to it. It's yours." He smiled. "That's all I wanted to tell you. I know it doesn't redeem me in any way, but… it's a start."

I looked at him. I really looked at him, and I thought I did see repent in his dark eyes. "You'll get there if you keep trying," I told him, knowing that everyone made mistakes - sometimes really terrible ones - but making them unforgivable simply meant that a person could never right the wrongs they'd done.

"Thanks, I will," he said and walked back through the crowds of packing up businesses.

Upon reflection, I thought the day had gone rather well.

That night, Auryn and I broke into the records room.

Ever since I'd happened upon Flannigan holding that file, I'd wondered if he'd been telling the truth. Had he really been going through zoo employees' personal records, or had he been looking at something else?

Tonight, I was determined to find out.

"How did you learn to pick locks again?" Auryn asked while I struggled to get the door to the records room open.

"YouTube. It's going to work," I assured both him and myself as I fiddled with my makeshift lock-breaking tools.

To both of our surprise, the lock clicked. I turned the handle and the door opened.

"You spend too much time with spies," Auryn told me before following me into the room.

I led the way to the filing cabinet Flannigan had been standing next to when he'd dropped the file and given himself away. The blank metal wasn't labelled in any way and gave no hint as to its contents.

I shrugged at Auryn and tugged hopefully on the top drawer. It didn't budge.

With a sigh, I assembled my tools for smaller locks whilst Auryn went to stand guard outside the room. I very much doubted that there were any late workers... but I was less convinced that we would avoid others who were staying late for more unscrupulous reasons. Those animals in the secret room still needed to be fed, and they could hardly be fed at sociable hours when potential witnesses were around.

I felt a jolt of elation when the lock gave up the ghost and I was able to slide the drawer out. My first impression when it was open was that I must be mistaken. This wasn't the records of employees. It was the records of all of the animals in the zoo. I flicked through, realising that they were sorted into quarterly reports, dating back from when the zoo had been founded. Every file contained an overall account of the numbers of different species of animals present in the zoo at the time of the report. Beyond that, where numbers had changed, there were reports from the zookeepers on which animals had been born or died.

It was a familiar system to me. Even though we kept our records digitally these days, everyone always kept a hardcopy as backup. Digital files could become corrupted or be accidentally deleted.

Although, paper records weren't immune either, I noted.

The file containing the most recent quarterly report was missing.

"What innocent reason could you have for taking that?" I quietly muttered, mentally hammering the final nail home in Flannigan's coffin. He hadn't been looking at employee records. He'd been gathering smuggling evidence of his own. The only thing I didn't know was whether he was covering his criminal associates' tracks... or seeking information for blackmail.

I bit my lip, wondering what it changed. I'd already known that Flannigan possessed a suspicious amount of prior knowledge about animal smuggling at zoos. I'd already suspected him of being the double agent and having his fingers in a lot of criminal pies. Unfortunately, a missing file didn't amount to proof of anything.

All I was certain of was that Flannigan was guilty of something... and perhaps guilty of everything.

Our reviews were due in the next day. Auryn and I stayed up incredibly late after our break-in session and exchanged notes on what we'd managed to glean during our relatively brief time at the huge zoo. It was an unusual experience for me to be rushing to meet a deadline. Usually, I was well ahead of schedule and delivered extra upon the agreed amount. This time was different.

"This will do, right?" I'd muttered when we went to hand in the final documents.

Auryn shrugged, which pretty much summed up my own feelings about Corbyn Manor's Zoo Experience.

It would do.

After the reviews had been handed in, we were both staying on for a few more days, which would hopefully offset any suspicion that we'd had anything to do with the changes that might come. To be frank, I wasn't convinced that our ruse of staying on would pay off. I knew full well that I had enemies at this place, and that they would surely strike against me in any way they could. I only hoped we could 'get the heck out of Dodge' before the lynch mob arrived.

All the same, I knew there were some elements of the zoo I would miss. One of these elements was Robyn. She was, in her own way, delightful, and I was going to sorely miss her. I'd even considered asking her to come and work at The Lucky Zoo where she would be much more appreciated, but I knew that the commute would be a long one for her. Perhaps when all was said and done, I'd tell her the truth, hope she'd forgive me, and then say there was always a job for her, should she ever want one. That would be the best thing, I decided.

When we returned home that night, I began the arduous task that was going over the zoo and restaurant's monthly financials. I employed an accountant to sort out both, but I would be a fool to not look over them myself.

I took a sip of my cinnamon-spiced hot chocolate and scanned the pages filled with numbers.

"Holy cow," I muttered and then said it again.

The wager I'd begun with Auryn over who would be in profit first was at an end.

"Well, how about that!" I said.

It was with a big grin on my face that I went downstairs and announced that we wouldn't be cooking tonight... we were going out to celebrate.

"What are we celebrating?" Auryn asked, grumpily, as I drove along the winding country roads. Usually, we didn't venture far beyond The Wild Spot in terms of eating out, but tonight was different. There was a sushi place a couple of towns over and tonight seemed as good a time as any to try it out.

"You'll see," I told him, maddeningly.

By the time we'd ordered, Auryn was just about ready to fling pickled ginger at me unless I told him what we were celebrating. I gave in and pulled out the financials.

"You're not going to believe this, but we both covered our costs and went into profit on the same day," I told him.

"Really? You're not just saying that so that you're not the loser?"

I rolled my eyes at him. "These are the real numbers! Come on, I'm not that sore a loser." I hesitated. "Would you have done that?!"

"Of course not!" Auryn grinned. "I'd have fiddled it so that I was the winner."

I slapped his hand with the chopsticks and then, mercifully, our food arrived before the grand inquisition could continue.

Inside, I knew I'd done the right thing by nudging the numbers just a little. In truth, the restaurant had surpassed the needed profit the night before The Lucky Zoo had done the same when it opened in the morning, but I'd decided that when it came to business matters, twelve hours difference was nothing. Anyway, the big Halloween bash I'd held at The Wild Spot after the Halloween fete had definitely helped a great deal in pushing past that final mile-marker.

"What were the consequences again?" I asked him with a smile.

Auryn pretended to look thoughtful. "I think we were competing for the honour of keeping the peacocks and Bernard. Seeing as we drew, I'm going to gracefully concede them to you…"

I laughed but then grew serious. "If I see any of them on my land again, I'll have them delivered directly to your office."

The peacocks and Bernard were not something to be joked about.

THE LEOPARD WHO CHANGED
HIS SPOTS

vengers assemble! I blithely thought to myself when I looked around the room. It was Tuesday night - the day the smuggling shipment was scheduled, and we were ready for action.

Auryn and I had passed a pleasant enough final day at the zoo with both of us claiming we were casualties of the report that had been submitted by the team who'd investigated the zoo. No one on Auryn's team had contested it or seemed sorry, but Robyn had told me she'd fight tooth and nail for justice when I'd let her know my fate. It had only made me feel that much worse for lying to her.

The days leading up to the mission had been quiet at the zoo. The crowds had died down after the Halloween rush, and the only drama had been when the Indian Runners had squeezed through a hole in their fence and done a runner. An elderly tiger had passed away, but with new cubs on the way, morale remained high. The circle of life continued.

The relaxed atmosphere meant that we were able to spend most of our time carefully engineering and planning for every eventuality - at least, I hoped we had. As I was the only person who had the right to be in the incubation room, most of the setup had been down to me.

The room didn't naturally lend itself to hiding places. In order to rectify this, I'd been moving a lot of stuff into the room over the past few days on the premise that the pet zone was going to be acting as an emergency incubator for a nearby zoo (The Lucky Zoo, actually) who had lost power, due to an electrical fault that would take a while to fix. Everyone had kept their fingers crossed that the fairly flimsy excuse would hold up and not be investigated too thoroughly, but so far, it seemed that it had.

Everything was going perfectly to plan.

"No one is going to rush in and try to save the day," Detective Gregory reminded us all right before we exited the ex-MI5 shed we'd commandeered for this operation. It wasn't the first time it had been said.

"Will everyone stop looking at me? I don't go looking for trouble! It just… sort of finds me," I finished, lamely.

I looked around the room at the team we'd assembled. Lowell, Detective Gregory, Officer Kelly, Officer Ernesto, Auryn, and myself. That was everyone who was going up against the great unknown smuggling operation. I hoped it was enough.

All the same, I couldn't help feeling that there was a mistake being made. Did I really know who to trust within our little group? Could a traitor be in our midst right this second?

My eyes darted from person to person as I silently evaluated the possibilities. Nothing jumped out at me, but the knock on the shed door nearly made me jump out of my skin.

"Come in," Lowell called, looking the least surprised.

I narrowed my eyes, realising that he'd clearly been expecting this extra visitor. Was this the first sign of treachery? Lowell knew I was looking. He shook his head minutely and strode over and opened the door when the knocker didn't enter.

Katya stood on the step with a sheepish expression on her face.

I looked between her and Lowell and then back again.

"I owe you a big apology," she said to me.

"No you don't," I automatically countered, having already accepted that our recent loss of trust and friendship was a result of my own lack of honesty with her over my source in all of this smuggling business.

"I do. I've been checking into everything you told me, courtesy of your source. It all checked out and I found much more, too. There is a lot of evidence to suggest that this smuggling operation is exactly as Joe Harvey claimed. It's countrywide and being covered up."

"Then it's all true," I said, having been wondering that since Joe had told me the first time. I'd thought he might have made the whole thing up just to persuade me to employ him for whatever devious ends he'd intended. When we'd uncovered the hidden animals and overheard the conversation about shipments going out, I'd started to believe. Sure, there was still the possibility that this was all there was to it - one zoo with a dark side - but I'd been buoyed with hope, and now Katya seemed to believe it was warranted.

"He really did change," I concluded marvelling at Joe's altered moral compass. I wondered what had persuaded him to do it and then decided I shouldn't walk down that path. It was all finished now anyway.

"If this all goes to plan and we're on the verge of uncovering a huge operation, what will happen to the animals?" Officer Kelly asked.

We all looked at her. Then everyone turned as one to face me.

I bit my lip. It was a question that had been playing on my mind for a long time. Say we did manage to crack the whole thing wide open and there were convictions and punishments and all wrongs were righted... what would be left? Corbyn Manor was a prime example of the potential fallout. Not only were some of its keepers implicated in this dark business, their superiors were, too. There was a chance that the chain of command went all the way to the top. If that tower came tumbling down, I knew who would suffer. It would be the other zookeepers and zoo staff, who'd just been doing their jobs.

Then there was the displaced animals to consider. If the operation was unwrapped, where would they all go - the ones who couldn't be traced back to their homes? There were zoos who would be able to take some of the animals in, but I was sure there would be a surplus, and I hated to think of the consequences that it might have for the lives of the animals we were supposed to be rescuing.

"I'll figure out a way," I said out loud, thinking of the money I had, and the money that would undoubtedly still come. These days, I was incredibly fortunate. If I could afford to put things right, I certainly would.

The night was dark when we first heard signs of movement. For hours, we'd been camped out in our various hiding places and viewpoints, aware that someone else may also scout the area before the time for the exchange came.

I was crouched next to Lowell behind a stack of incubator boxes, arranged so that there was enough gap for us to see anyone who walked through the room and take photos of them in action. It was far from a safe hiding place, and although I'd wanted to stay far away from the action (proving I meant it about not looking for trouble) Katya had decreed that Lowell shouldn't be on his own. It had then been discovered that anyone taller than I was couldn't squeeze into such a small space with Lowell already taking up the lion's share of the room. I'd argued that I would hardly be of any help if we were discovered, but Katya had just rolled her eyes and given me a crash course with her gun. "Beginner's luck will be on your side, but I hope that you don't have to use it," she'd said.

I'd nodded dutifully and stashed it in the waist holster she'd lent me, feeling its alien weight against my thigh. I wasn't too convinced that I'd hit anything, should the need arise, and I prayed that it would be plain sailing from here.

But even I couldn't have predicted just how terribly wrong about that I would prove to be.

Lowell's squeeze on my arm alerted me to what I already knew. They were here.

The footsteps and voices arrived in the room. It was time.

"Buyer's late. No surprise there," I heard Taylor say. I felt some grim satisfaction that the animal welfare man was present. He'd been playing a lot of people for fools - myself included - and I would be happy when retribution came a-knocking.

"No reason for us to be late," Jennifer primly replied. She barked out some orders. I watched the couple in charge of the fowl at the zoo, and Winnie, the primate keeper, walk past my view point. Amphibian keeper, Kel, was close behind. Then, to my surprise, Rosa, the nastiest of the big cat keepers, followed. It was the first thing that made me feel a twinge of alarm. There'd been no sign of any big cats in the secret room when I'd last looked. I'd thought that - in spite of their rudeness - they weren't a part of the smuggling - or at least not involved in this particular shipment. There were no cubs available. I wondered if there was something I was missing.

The whole gang was here. Now all we needed was to obtain evidence that a deal had taken place.

Lowell was already recording everything that was happening in the room. As I turned my head slightly towards him, I saw him snapping some surreptitious shots with a tiny camera.

We could have bugged the room, but Lowell had reasoned that it wasn't nearly as foolproof as it appeared to be in the films. After all - if your spy gear went down whilst you were remotely viewing something, you could hardly pop into the room and fix it.

"Oh! You're here," Taylor said, sounding surprised. "Good. You can inspect the goods." I heard him push open the door in the wall that led to the secret room.

I discovered I was holding my breath, waiting for the mysterious buyer to walk into my view.

I wasn't sure what I was expecting, but she certainly wasn't it.

The woman I could see through the gap between boxes looked formidable. She was dressed in a dark steel power suit and her hair was held up high on her head in a fancy bun that I was more than willing to believe she'd paid someone to do for her. But it was her face that scared me when I caught a glimpse of her eyes. She was merciless.

"The goods will be up to scratch, or you will take a cut. Load in," she said, before spinning around on her stiletto heels and marching back towards the door.

A high screeching cut through the subdued atmosphere in the incubation room. I heard a slew of swearwords and then something tawny streaked out of the open secret door and past our hiding place, followed by a second fast-moving form. There was the sound of glass smashing.

"Get them back!" I heard Jennifer call. The lady in stilettos made a sound of disgust, but I didn't hear the door open. It proved she was every bit as sharp as she looked.

All around us, mayhem and screeching erupted. Incubators fell to the ground and people shouted, as the monkeys wreaked havoc with no restraint, until the inevitable happened. The monkeys found us.

First, there was the curious face poking over the top of the wall of boxes we'd concealed ourselves behind. Then, the screeching cry came when the Rhesus monkey decided we were more interesting than aggravating its would-be captors.

With a rage-filled screech, it dropped down and landed on Lowell's head, behaving in the spiteful manner I'd witnessed many times from primates in zoos. Monkeys and apes could be wonderfully intelligent and compassionate creatures, but get one in a bad mood and you would be sorry.

Lowell reached for his gun when the monkey sank its teeth into his ear. I desperately lunged to still his instinctive movement. The gun stayed silent. However, the thrashing around had been enough to cause our precarious screen to tumble to the ground. We were fully exposed to the smuggling gang… and their guns were all pointing our way.

"I warned you," Taylor hissed, turning a little to face Jennifer.

Jennifer just stood there with her mouth agape.

"Is there something I should know about these two eavesdroppers?" The intimidating woman asked, her voice sweet and drenched in danger.

"Yes. Jennifer employed a famous comic-book author and professional snooper to spy on the zoo. Now she's surprised that she's rumbled our operation," Taylor said with a shake of his head.

"What about the other?" She looked at Lowell, and I saw something thoughtful on her face. She considered him to be far more interesting than I was. I could live with that. Being underestimated was something that had helped me more than once in tough spots.

"Oh... he's with the police," Jennifer said with the utmost certainty.

"The police?" The woman was frowning now.

"Yeah, they came here to keep an eye on her because she received a death threat, or something. We had to pretend to employ them to do the job that she was actually doing." Jennifer shrugged like it was no big deal.

"He's not with the police," the woman said, looking at Lowell again. "They were onto us from the start." She raised her gun a little higher, pointing it straight between Lowell's eyes. "I'll let you live... if you tell me who your source was." Her voice was sticky and sweet with the promise of salvation. I knew as well as Lowell surely did that she was lying. This woman was not someone who would allow someone to spy on her and let them live to tell the tale. I also wasn't convinced that Jennifer would be safe. She didn't seem to realise it, but I was certain there would be a price to pay for what she'd done.

I'm afraid I didn't feel very sorry for her.

"Our source was murdered," I said, figuring playing for time was as good as it got. With a bit of luck, the others stationed outside the building would realise something was wrong and come steaming in, guns blazing.

The woman looked unimpressed. "How convenient."

"He used to work for a gang of money launderers. Perhaps you heard of him?" Lowell continued, catching my drift.

"We will have moved in very different circles. Money movers are a different breed." There was something ugly that passed across her face in that moment. I wondered about it, before remembering that we were in mortal peril. All of my mental power should be dedicated towards figuring out how to not get shot.

The woman glanced down at the ornate watch on her wrist. "You're making me late," she stated, and then, as if it were as simple a decision as taking a breath, I watched her pull the trigger.

Lowell was already in motion even as I stood there with my mouth hanging open like a complete fool. He hit me hard and we crashed to the ground, scattering the boxes everywhere. My shoulder hit the floor with a painful crack, but the sound the bullet made when it sailed over our heads and embedded itself in the wall certainly made my shoulder feel like a much better alternative. Lowell rolled off me as soon as we landed. I was left gasping for air on the ground as he sprang into action, taking the gun out of my holster, ready to fight for our lives.

"MI5! Stop right where you are. You're surrounded!" a loud voice shouted out. All at once, a sea of black figures ran into the room. The escaped monkeys howled and screamed, but they seemed just as alarmed by the appearance of all these people as I was, and they backed off into a corner.

With a look that promised a painful death, if she ever got a chance to inflict it, the woman lowered her gun. Her underlings mirrored the movement. The door to the secret room swung open, and with comic timing, Rosa, Winnie, Kel, Bill and Freya walked out, carrying animals that were definitely not supposed to be leaving the zoo.

"You're under arrest," Detective Gregory said, striding into the room and grabbing the keepers with the help of Officer Ernesto and Officer Kelly. The MI5 agents eyed him with mistrust, and I even thought I heard one of them mutter a name I didn't recognise. The detective glared around, daring anyone to step forward.

The tension broke when Ms Borel and Mr Flannigan

entered the room. Dressed in their preferred attire of suits, they both had a smug look of satisfaction on their faces.

"How did you know to come here?" I asked, immediately suspecting Lowell, or even Katya, of telling tales. How convinced by Katya's apology was I? She might have wanted to enact some of her own justice. Or perhaps she'd used me from the start.

"Our purpose at this zoo wasn't a single one, as you may have believed. We received some new intelligence that illegal smuggling was happening at this location. We've known for a long time that it's been happening to some extent. Every now and then we like to make a raid to remind them that we're always watching. They won't get away with it forever," Flannigan said with a casual shrug.

I tried to digest what he was saying. "You know people smuggle animals and you occasionally bust them… but you never do anything more? You've been letting this carry on?"

Ms Borel looked at me as if I were a particularly bothersome mosquito who kept buzzing around her head. "We are busy and don't have the time or resources to dedicate to it. Sometimes, you have to pick the worst of the bad bunch and target them. Only then can you turn your gaze further down the ladder."

"Then why not ask someone else to do it? This was supposed to be an evidence gathering mission. We wanted to take down the whole operation. I wanted to," I quietly corrected, knowing I'd practically coerced the people around me into it. And all because of a wanted criminal who'd genuinely changed his affiliation.

Flannigan shook his head at me, looking faintly amused. "That's not the way the world works." He made a motion with his hand and more agents rushed in and seized the arrested keepers, who had been in the care of Alex Gregory.

"We need them to further our investigations. I'm sure you understand."

The look on Detective Gregory's face said he did... but he was not happy about it in the least.

"Well! I think that just about wraps it up," Flannigan announced, clapping his hands together. "Don't worry about the lorry you lot left outside either, that's also in our care," he told the captured criminals.

"But what about the animals?" I piped up.

Flannigan stared at me like I'd just announced I would be performing the can-can in the nude. "Sorry?"

"The animals. Some of them won't be in the zoo's system. You said there's a lorry outside. Are there animals in there?"

Flannigan shrugged to say he didn't know. *What a surprise.*

"Who's going to take care of them? There's no guarantee the zoos will take them back. There'll be no record of the animals existing, or they'll have been registered as deceased. You already know that," I added, before biting my tongue. Now wasn't the time to make a move on Flannigan. Not when he held all of the cards. My case against the double agent was still suffering from a severe lack of evidence. "I know I'd be hesitant to take an animal whose history I wasn't quite sure of," I continued, hoping he'd missed my slip-up. "For example, if one of the animals was carrying a disease, it could spread to other animals. So... what's going to happen to them?"

There was a lot of foot shuffling.

"They'll be quarantined, I suppose," Ms Borel said, stepping in when her colleague failed her. The 'I suppose' bit did little to placate me.

"They'll disappear. It's always the easy option to destroy animals, and it's not necessary!"

"What's your solution?" Mrs Borel asked with cool detachment.

"I'll take them," I said without hesitation. "I've got the space, and the money. I can erect a quarantine zone in no time at all and build permanent enclosures as soon as possible." I knew it wasn't ideal, but at least it was better than the dark unknowns of the alternative.

Ms Borel sniffed. "Fine. I'll see if that is acceptable to the relevant authorities." And just like that, the idea I'd had ever since Drew James had let me know about the extra land I owned took its first step towards being a reality.

"Clear out!" Flannigan barked, startling the team in black into action. "You are all coming, too. I'm sure I don't have to tell you that for some of you..." he eyeballed Katya, Lowell, and Detective Gregory each in turn "...there will be disciplinary action taken for involving civilians and breaking your cover. We had this sting operation covered. You are fortunate that no one was injured. Now... out!"

I had to bite my lip from accusing him right there and then of being a two-faced liar.

"Ahem!" Ms Borel cleared her throat. "I see there are two primates loose. For ease of cleanup they should be returned to confinement." It was with a sinking heart that I discovered she was looking at me.

"Right," I said, turning to Auryn. He shrugged back in return. We had got ourselves into this situation by offering to take on all of the wayward animals. This was probably just desserts.

We watched the monkeys until everyone had cleared out of the room, and we were finally alone with the two escapees.

"I feel so mean trying to get them back into a tiny cage," I commented, circling around to try to get the measure of the pair.

"They'll be happier soon. You're doing something to save them," Auryn reassured me. He'd supported the idea from the start when I'd had my blinding flash of inspiration.

"How the heck are we going to catch them?" I murmured. The two Rhesus monkeys stared back at me as if daring me to try it. They were out, and they weren't going back in without a fight - that much was obvious.

"Try food?" Auryn asked and then prodded my back pocket.

"Hey!" I complained.

He rolled his eyes. "I know that's not your leg. You have stakeout snacks."

"There aren't many left," I protested, taking out the packet of jellybeans I'd concealed in my pocket to pass the time whilst waiting for the bad guys to turn up. "They're bad for them!" I weakly protested, but Auryn just shot me a quelling look. There was a time and a place for worrying about animals' dental hygiene. Now wasn't it.

I sprinkled the remainder of the packet inside the cage, picking up a few to tempt them over, and a few more in case only one monkey walked in the first time. Then, with careful aim, I tossed two beans towards the watching monkeys.

"Ah..."

Auryn raised his gaze heavenwards and then walked forwards a couple of paces to where the beans had dropped short. Okay, so maybe I'd misjudged it a little. He tossed them onwards. This time they bounced at the monkeys' feet.

We held our breath.

One of the monkeys reached out and picked up the colourful bean. For a moment, it considered the foreign object, flaring its nostrils. After a second of indecision, it popped it in its mouth.

With a whooping cry, it reached for the other bean, but its monkey companion had also been watching the careful testing and tasting. An argument broke out over the bean and the situation was only resolved when I rattled the handful inside of their cage.

Both monkeys turned… and then they ran, racing one another to get to the colourful bounty. I shut the door behind them with a sigh of relief. "That was a lot easier than I'd anticipated."

Auryn looked surprised. "I know! We never seem to catch a break. I guess we must have deserved one after all this time."

A loud snarl set the monkeys chattering and caused general bedlam in the secret room.

Auryn and I looked at one another.

"What the heck was that?" I said. As one, we walked into the secret room to discover what new animal had been added to the shipment.

There was a tiger in the shipping container.

I knew it by scent before we even saw its amber eyes watching us through the air holes.

"It makes sense now," I murmured, remembering that an old tiger had supposedly passed away in recent days. Rosa, and perhaps her colleagues, too, had pretended to kill off one of their tigers, so that it could be shipped off to a buyer. I was sickened by the thought of how many times it might have happened before now, and the fate of those unfortunate animals.

"He'll be safe with us," Auryn said, knowing exactly what to say.

I sighed. "This has all gone wrong. They're all acting like we should be happy, being saved and seeing the bad guys caught, but it's the tip of the iceberg - and they know it! Why can't they support people who want to stop this dreadful trade, if they're stretched too thinly themselves to do anything about it?"

"We can only do what we can do," Auryn said, looking sadly at the tiger in the box. "No one can save them all."

"But we can try," I reasoned.

Auryn's jaw set in a hard line. "We certainly can."

And just like that, I knew we weren't going to give up the fight. MI5 may have damaged our journey towards the truth tonight by putting a tiny dent in a much larger operation, but that was no reason to stop fighting. We were going to do everything in our power to put a stop to the dark smuggling trade that was rotting away at the heart of the zoos in Britain.

"Anything I can do to right his wrongs," Auryn said. I knew he was talking about his father. This mission of ours had hit close to home and evidently reminded him of the man he'd grown up respecting, only to have the illusion shattered. It had forced Auryn to become the man he was today. While I believed he had become a wonderful man, there was a large part of me that still wished he'd been given the chance to grow up a little more slowly.

It was the sound of a safety catch being clicked off that alerted us to the presence in the room.

"I've waited a long time for this moment."

Ms Borel stood in the doorway with a gun pointed directly between us.

A MENAGERIE OF MADNESS

For a second, no one spoke. But then, seemingly freed from the sludge that had been dragging it down, the wheels in my brain started to turn.

"It's you. It's always been you," I said, scarcely able to believe how wrong I'd been.

"Why?" Auryn looked just as baffled as I felt.

"Money, power, and an altruistic desire to do good. Why else?" Ms Borel came as close to actually smiling as I'd ever seen her.

"You call this doing good?" Auryn gestured around.

She shook her head. "I have nothing to do with these pond scum. They're just a convenient cover-up and a means to an end. My allegiance is with your old publishing friends. Or at least, some of them." Steel flashed in her eyes when she said it. "The powers-that-be condemn their actions for helping terrorism and aiding in corruption. But I see a better economy and changes that require force to be welcomed in. That term 'terrorist' is thrown around far too lightly these days. But I'll spare you the ideological discussion. We need to keep this short and sweet." She hesitated. "Well, not so sweet... but you know that."

"Why murder Joe?" I could see it all now. She'd known where we kept the ladders, and she'd known everything about the publishing contract - and apparently Joe's new identity.

She tutted. "Because he was changing sides and he knew too much. The longer he stayed with you, the more likely it got that he'd tell you the truth, instead of playing by the rules. He had to go. With my contacts, I knew he was snooping around the animal smugglers this country is so excellent at harbouring, and I knew about the lynx they'd lost and you'd found. It was the perfect cover."

"You tried to frame me!" I said, realising it was as I'd suspected - a set-up. "Did you send the death threat, too?"

"That was MI5 sanctioned to try to bring my comrades out of hiding believing that you knew something. Obviously, I informed my friends that you had no idea at all... but one of them didn't take my word for it. I thought she might be straying from the flock..." She tutted. "If only I'd employed a more competent clean-up crew."

I remembered the meeting with Leona and the appearance of the gun-toting men. Had it been a triple attempted murder?

"I thought it was Flannigan," I muttered, feeling like a fool.

Ms Borel grinned like a crocodile before dinnertime. "That bumbling idiot! He even got caught by you taking that file out of the records room. The fool thought he was helping the investigation. In fact, he was giving me everything I needed for a spot of blackmail, should the need have arisen. Those records hadn't been modified yet. It would have been very awkward if they'd resurfaced later." She shook her head.

"I didn't count on Flannigan organising this ridiculous sting, rather than taking my suggestion and waiting it out to see if we could catch the bigger fish." She looked speculatively at us. "I think we were on the same side there. I don't like to get involved with the bottom feeders. Tipping them off is beneath me. However, I had hoped that you would make an error and end up dead." She shrugged. "This is less convenient, but I'll make it work."

"But Flannigan already knew about the animal smuggling when I found him in the records room," I said, still trying to reason that this couldn't be the truth.

Ms Borel rolled her eyes. "I was the one who told him. I claimed there was some new intel that smugglers were operating at this zoo, and then I sent him on his way to get the record I needed, knowing he would keep tabs on you and work for the company with loyalty and without asking questions." She looked amused.

I'd already digressed in my mind. "Sorrel... sounds like... Borel," I muttered, shaking my head as it finally all made sense. Joe hadn't been laying on the drama, he'd been acting out a clue.

If he were still alive today, I'd have strangled him.

"I think you're doing it all because you're looking out for yourself. You don't care about doing good." I should have remembered that goading people holding loaded guns pointed your way is never a good idea.

"I think it's time for you to die," she said, raising the gun.

"You can't shoot us with that gun. It's one issued by MI5. They'll know it was you," Auryn protested, spouting something that sounded like half-remembered action film knowledge.

I looked hopefully back and forth between them, wondering if we would get out of this on a technicality that Ms Borel had overlooked. I doubted it.

"I'm head of operations. No one is going to question me when I report that you were working with the smugglers all along. I've already sown the seeds of doubt in Flannigan's mind. Why do you think he questioned you about the smugglers when you caught him in the records room? Plus, you've admitted to colluding with a known criminal. Providing evidence would be a simple matter." She looked annoyed that she'd been derailed enough to bother explaining to two people condemned to die. "However... it would be quite inconvenient. That's why you're going to let that tiger out."

I turned to look behind us at the amber eyes that were watching our every move. I knew from cold hard experience that tigers at the zoo were far from tame. Even if it was just curiosity and not malice, it would be a terrible end for Auryn and me.

"Open it," she barked.

We hesitated.

"Or I'll just shoot you," she drawled.

I wasn't sure which was better. A quick death by gunshot, or taking our chances with an equally deadly tiger.

"Hopefully they already fed him," I muttered to Auryn as we walked back towards the box. Unfortunately, I knew that hunger didn't have much to do with whether we lived or died. For all their wildness, tigers shared a lot of traits with their domestic cousins. Much like cats, they would seize any chance to hunt smaller squeakier things than themselves. Like humans.

Ms Borel backed up to the door. She wasn't going to be hanging around for the show. A small spark of hope flared inside me. Once we'd let the tiger out, all we had to do was get out of reach or find a way to escape, and we could ride this out.

With a despairing look at one another, and then back at

the gun barrel still directed our way, Auryn and I lifted the wooden bar across the box's door and undid the top catch.

The tiger lurched out. Ms Borel shut the door with a final slam. We were left to our doom.

It was only later that I'd come to recall hearing someone scream, but at the time, it hardly seemed important.

For a moment, time stood still. Auryn, the tiger, and I stood together in a space that felt terribly confined. All around us, the animals in their cages were going crazy at the sight and smell of the tiger on the loose. It didn't matter whether or not they'd seen a tiger before, they all knew it was a predator.

"Quick! In the box," Auryn said, seeing our chance when the tiger was momentarily distracted by the number of available quarries. We darted inside. It was as we reached out to pull the door back up that the tiger figured it out. We weren't behind glass or bars. We were right there and moving in such a prey-like way.

With a grunt it turned and launched itself at us.

The wood bent inwards and then rebounded. It nearly took my fingernails with it as Auryn and I struggled to hold the wooden door up. We'd made it inside the box, but there was no way to shut it from the inside. Our fingers were the only thing keeping the door in place. I said a silent prayer of thanks that tigers had been born without opposable thumbs.

I'd forgotten about their claws.

With a horrible raking sound, four claws as big as knives were hooked over the top of the door. Auryn and I held on for as long as our fingers would let us, but the tiger had embedded itself in the wood, and what match were we for the strength of a full-grown tiger?

As one, we let go, knowing that this was it. This was how it all ended. I reached out for Auryn's hand, and he for mine, as the door came down. I reflected that, as ends went, this was probably a fitting one. I'd lived my life trying to help animals engage with their wildest instincts and live wild lives. Now I was about to pay the price for finally getting too close. At least I'd followed my heart.

The tiger's eyes seemed to glint with victory until, with a puzzled growl, it slumped sideways onto the ground.

Lowell stood behind it with a tranquilliser gun pressed to his shoulder and a grim look on his face.

"You saved us!" *And the tiger,* I silently added, thrilled that the animal would survive the ordeal. I would never blame him for attacking us. It was simple instinct.

"How did you know?" Auryn asked, and then frowned. "And where's Ms Borel?"

A grim look of satisfaction appeared on Lowell's face. "She stepped on a snake."

"What kind?" I immediately asked.

"Black mamba, so I'd watch where you tread," Lowell said, fixing me with a thoughtful look for a moment.

I shuddered, brought back to my time at Snidely Safari where I'd gotten way too up close and personal with a lot of the same variety of snake. I knew just how deadly they could be.

"It must have got out when the monkeys were loose and smashed the place up," I said, thinking back to the bedlam before our discovery.

Lowell nodded. "She's been taken to hospital with an escort and is already receiving emergency medical treatment. If she pulls through, you can bet the full weight of the law will be thrown at her." He hefted the tranquilliser gun up onto his shoulder now that the tiger was subdued. "I figured it out as soon as I realised Ms Borel was gone. I've worked with her ever since I was recruited from that gun smuggling case. Even back then, I was surprised to be head-hunted by her, because who could have known I was working the case?

I've been putting it down to the secret service being secretive all these years, but really, it was probably because the bad guys tipped her off that I was someone worth watching. Keep your enemies close."

"But how did you put it together?" I pressed.

Now Lowell looked guilty for a second. "With your help, mostly. I've always denied that there could be anyone working as a double agent, but you seemed so sure, and it must have got to me. To be honest, I was watching for it. When I realised Ms Borel had disappeared... I just knew it had to be her. It's strange, I think I considered everyone but her. She seemed above suspicion. Perfect record and all that." He shrugged.

"The perfect thing to hide behind," Auryn observed.

We all looked down at the tiger.

"Who wants to help me get him back into the box?" I asked.

Surprisingly, I wasn't overwhelmed by offers.

"You'll be in a new home soon," I promised the sleeping tiger after we'd collected the others from the disarrayed MI5 and I'd coerced Lowell, Auryn, Katya, and the Gigglesfield police force representatives into helping me manoeuvre the big cat back into its small holding cell.

"What are you going to call your quarantine zoo?" Katya asked as the relevant authorities showed up to start taking note of the animals present and were told that there would be a place for any who couldn't be returned.

"Monday's Menagerie," I told her. It had finally felt like the right name.

I turned to my companions, feeling a smile light up my face as I looked around. All of them were my friends, and all of us had come so far together. I knew there were still tough times ahead if we wanted to right the wrongs on our crusade against the animal smugglers, but I knew that, somehow, we would pull it off.

It may not change the world in some big, noticeable way, but it would save some animals from suffering. The world would be a little better for it. And that was all I'd ever wanted.

EPILOGUE

I n the aftermath of the smuggling bust, a lot of things changed. Taylor Morningstar and Jennifer Bucket were prosecuted along with their zookeeper accomplices. Corbyn Manor's Zoo Experience had shown its true colours by refusing to acknowledge any of the good work that had been done to stop the rot in their own ranks. Instead, the zoo had repeated its 'no tolerance' policy over and over, seeming to believe that a policy meant that smuggling was now an impossibility. On the bright side, Robyn hadn't been angry when I'd revealed the truth to her and she'd since started work at both The Lucky Zoo and Avery setting up an ethical petting zone - one she promised I wouldn't hate.

Ms Borel pulled through after being very hastily administered anti-venom at hospital. British Intelligence were thoroughly ashamed to have been harbouring someone like Ms Borel amongst their ranks. Katya informed me that the head of operations had been prosecuted but had made a deal to sell out her old money laundering friends for a lighter sentence. Even though she'd allegedly sung like a canary, the group had slipped through their fingers again, raising further questions about possible infiltration. I'd been unsurprised that Ms Borel hadn't turned out to be as steadfast and loyal to the 'right cause' as she'd claimed. It was evident that she was a hardhearted woman who would do just about anything, if it benefited her.

Whilst I'd kept in contact with Katya and Lowell as we'd worked to crack the smuggling ring, after the initial bust, my dealings with British Intelligence had happily fizzled out. One year later, I hadn't had to put up with any undercover operatives snooping around, or been visited by the irritating Mr Flannigan - whom I'd heard had retired soon after Ms Borel was found guilty.

There had been several legal loopholes to jump through, in order to become a registered facility that was able to quarantine animals a safe distance from other animals and observe all the protocols. I'd contracted Georgina Farley to do the job. She'd come through in spectacular fashion as she always did. Our winning argument had been that there simply weren't any facilities dedicated to dealing with the smuggling crises. Quarantines were kept small to house occasional residents - usually animals shipped between zoos. This was a large scale problem that had needed a lot of housing. It hadn't taken long to set up temporary enclosures for all of the animals seized during the first bust, and not long after that, a more permanent set-up had been arranged. When animals were deemed safe and healthy, new homes were found for them at reputable zoos. However, a good number of them remained at The Lucky Zoo and at Avery, and that was just fine.

Even though I'd had money to start up the menagerie, we set a trust up when things started to look tight. I am still overwhelmed by the amount people are willing to give to support a cause that I believe so strongly in.

As for the smugglers, we were still coming for them. Five

successful busts had been carried out since the first one, where Auryn and I had nearly been mauled to death.

As well as actively seeking them out, we'd also managed to arrange an amnesty. Anyone with illegally obtained animals or animals that were earmarked for the trade could hand them in at Monday's Menagerie with no questions asked. I'd been surprised by the success rate of this offer, and also surprised by the variety of animals that had been brought in. The elephant had definitely knocked me for six.

Several new quarantine blocks had needed to be built, and I was still doing everything in my power to make sure the animals in our care had the best lives we could give them until they found new homes.

Lucky had managed to sneak across to the quarantine zone when I hadn't been looking. The keeper on duty had attached a string to his harness and had walked him through the quarantine on her rounds. Lucky had been curious about all of the animals in their temporary homes, but had soon got the idea that he had to keep his distance. In spite of that, the keeper had reported that animals who hadn't been eating prior to Lucky's visit had developed appetites soon after. My black and white cat now took himself off to visit the quarantine whenever I went into The Lucky Zoo with him, and he'd continued to make a difference by boosting morale in a mysterious animal way that I couldn't fathom. Seeing him help other animals always brought a tear to my eye. It made me think back to a time, what felt like an age ago, when he'd been a tiny kitten rejected by his mother. Every day I was reminded of what a great choice it had been to save him.

Apart from the days when he hid dead things in our bed. Then it was a different story…

Part of me still wondered if I'd become the very thing I hated - a spy. But I thought the difference lay in my reasoning behind it. I knew there were lines I would never cross. I would never toy with someone's feelings, and I would never take advantage of an innocent bystander or manipulate them in order to catch the smugglers. Everything we did was made possible by a lot of good will and perseverance.

One year on, the smugglers were running scared and their business had dwindled. A lot of zoos had been ordered to fire anyone involved with the trade and clean up their acts, but although it had a knock-on effect on some of their loyal staff, who saw their jobs disappear when zoos folded, sometimes you needed to cut away more than just the rot you could see in order to save the tree. Anyway - I was always there to help them get back on their feet. It was another element that the Monday's Menagerie Trust funded.

I was flattered and amazed to find my name listed in the Birthday Honours in June, and had since received an OBE for services both to animals and to literature. It was an honour I'd been thrilled to accept, and it had only increased my resolve to improve the lives of animals in every way I possibly could.

My second comic book was a roaring success, and my ear already has a flea in it over just when I'm going to finish the manuscript for the third. Gloria has always proclaimed how much she loves the fact that I'm considered a national hero these days, but she doesn't seem to think that saving animals should take up so much of my time. She's only doing her job, and the comic is nearly finished, so then there'll be a brief period of quiet before I suppose they'll want another one.

My comic's success still doesn't feel quite real to me. The webcomic, however, is still going as strong as ever, and plenty of new and exotic characters have worked their way into the storyline to play with Lucky and Rameses.

Nothing ever came of the big film deal in Hollywood for my life's story, and I was glad of it. However, a smaller company did pitch to create a cartoon featuring Lucky and

Rameses. After I'd approved it, the series was made faster than I'd been able to believe. So far, the reviews were good, and I enjoyed watching their antics on screen.

Tonight I was sitting watching the pilot for the second season of *Rameses and Lucky*. Lucky had decided to be a sociable cat tonight and was curled across the back of the sofa with his tail tickling my neck. To my left, Rameses opened his mouth wide in a yawn and went back to sleep, oblivious to his cartoon version on the TV, who was currently being tricked into doing wrong by the conniving Lucky.

I took a moment to reflect upon how happy I was. Things had gone quiet on the smuggling front after our last big raid, and there was a certain stillness to the air that I always associated with the late autumn. I was happily married, with friends I loved, and with a zoo and a comic that both continued to be remarkably successful. I was even able to use some of that success to help animals in trouble.

Life was pretty perfect. And yet… I knew I had an itch I couldn't scratch, somewhere inside me.

I was still thinking on that when Auryn walked in, having returned from a club meeting with the much-reformed Lords of the Downs.

"Hey, I got a call from someone in Scotland. He said he's the new manager of a zoo that's supposed to be successful and reputable, but he reckons that none of the staff have a clue what they're doing, and the animals are looking worse by the day. He was wondering if we still worked as zoo consultants?" Auryn raised his eyebrows at me. For a whole year, we'd focused on breaking open the smuggling ring. Everything else that had happened had been secondary. We were both fortunate to have excellent teams of people left behind to run our zoos whilst we'd focused on our animal saving mission. I didn't regret a single moment, but seeing as things had been quiet for a while now...

"He sounded desperate," Auryn added, sitting down next to me on the sofa and receiving a good washing from Rameses.

"Well, in that case..." I said, knowing that I couldn't conceal my smile any longer. Somewhere inside, I felt the itch vanish. "It's a pretty simple case, isn't it?"

Auryn nodded sincerely. "Nothing could possibly go wrong."

BOOKS IN THE SERIES

Penguins and Mortal Peril

The Silence of the Snakes

Murder is a Monkey's Game

Lions and the Living Dead

The Peacock's Poison

A Memory for Murder

Whales and a Watery Grave

Chameleons and a Corpse

Foxes and Fatal Attraction

Monday's Murderer

Prequel: Parrots and Payback

A REVIEW IS WORTH ITS WEIGHT IN GOLD!

I really hope you enjoyed reading this story. I was wondering if you could spare a couple of moments to rate and review this book? As an indie author, one of the best ways you can help support my dream of being an author is to leave me a review on your favourite online book store, or even tell your friends.

Reviews help other readers, just like you, to take a chance on a new writer!

Thank you!
Ruby Loren

ALSO BY RUBY LOREN

HOLLY WINTER MYSTERIES

Snowed in with Death

A Fatal Frost

Murder Beneath the Mistletoe

Winter's Last Victim

EMILY HAVERSSON OLD HOUSE MYSTERIES

The Lavender of Larch Hall

The Leaves of Llewellyn Keep

The Snow of Severly Castle

The Frost of Friston Manor

The Heart of Heathley House

HAYLEY ARGENT HORSE MYSTERIES

The Swallow's Storm

The Starling's Summer

The Falcon's Frost

The Waxwing's Winter

JANUARY CHEVALIER SUPERNATURAL MYSTERIES

Death's Dark Horse

Death's Hexed Hobnobs

Death's Endless Enchanter

Death's Ethereal Enemy

Death's Last Laugh

Prequel: Death's Reckless Reaper

BLOOMING SERIES

Blooming

Abscission

Frost-Bitten

Blossoming

Flowering

Fruition

Made in United States
North Haven, CT
06 August 2022

22355977R00136